What the critics are saying...

5 Roses for Miss February! "I never walked away from reading this book. I enjoyed it so much that I read it twice…I enjoyed that Miss February was about a woman who was not perfect for we are not in a perfect world." ~ *A Romance Review*

Recommended Read for Miss December! "The characters of Miss December grabbed me from the first. Both believe they are an anomaly, misfits in their world…I could not put this book down. Madison Hayes is to be commended for her work. I would highly recommend this novel, and I cannot wait to read more from her." ~ *The Road to Romance*

Silver Star Award for Miss April! "Miss Hayes has once again hit just the right tone with this story…but be warned, this is a story that engages all of your emotions. I cried, laughed and lusted, and felt betrayed right along with these two, which is why I feel Miss April is definitely deserving of the Silver Star Award." ~ *Just Erotic Romance Reviews*

Flavor of the Month

Madison Hayes

An Ellora's Cave Romantica Publication

www.ellorascave.com

Flavor of the Month

ISBN 1419955187

Edited by Mary Moran and Pamela Campbell
Cover art by Syneca

Trade paperback Publication July 2006

Warning:

The following material contains graphic sexual content meant for mature readers. This story has been rated E–rotic by a minimum of three independent reviewers.

Ellora's Cave Publishing offers three levels of Romantica™ reading entertainment: S (S-ensuous), E (E-rotic), and X (X-treme).

S-*ensuous* love scenes are explicit and leave nothing to the imagination.

E-*rotic* love scenes are explicit, leave nothing to the imagination, and are high in volume per the overall word count. In addition, some E-rated titles might contain fantasy material that some readers find objectionable, such as bondage, submission, same sex encounters, forced seductions, and so forth. E-rated titles are the most graphic titles we carry; it is common, for instance, for an author to use words such as "fucking", "cock", "pussy", and such within their work of literature.

X-*treme* titles differ from E-rated titles only in plot premise and storyline execution. Unlike E-rated titles, stories designated with the letter X tend to contain controversial subject matter not for the faint of heart.

Also by Madison Hayes

ꟙ

Alpha Romeos
Dye's Kingdom: Wanting It Forever
Enter the Dragon (*anthology)*
Gryffin Strain: His Female
Kingdom of Khal: Redeeming Davik
Kingdom of Yute: Tor's Betrayal
Made for Two Men
Zeke's Hands

Contents

Dedication

...to Pam, editor extraordinaire

Miss February

ꟈ

Chapter One

ꝏ

"Do me a favor?" His voice was a rich, deep rumble.

Callie smiled into the phone, savoring the sound of that voice. "Anything," she answered automatically, knowing he would expect it and figuring she had a rough idea of what he would request. Her divorce had just been finalized and he could probably tell she was feeling low. He'd probably say something sweet and corny like "keep your head up, beautiful". Bret was like that.

She shook her head. Bret alone of all her friends had advised her against marrying Richard. Everyone else, including her entire family, had congratulated her on her engagement as though she'd scored a major coup. She, herself, had thought she'd never get a better offer—never get *another* offer for that matter. Her marriage to Richard had been a mistake from the start. She hadn't loved him—there'd always been something missing.

"Spend the weekend in Hawaii with me."

She almost dropped the phone. There were a few moments of silence while she waited for him to follow this with some kind of punch line.

"Come on, Callie," he pleaded with the laughing, wheedling tone he'd been using on her since they were kids. "I won a free trip at the office Christmas party." She heard some papers rustle in the background. "All expense paid Valentine's Weekend in Hawaii…for two."

"I don't know, Bret," she said in a voice that probably revealed just how low she was feeling. Normally, she was a sucker for Bret's charm.

"You'd be doing me a big favor," he said, haltingly. "You see... I didn't want to tell you...but I was in an accident a few weeks ago—"

"Bret! Are you all right?"

"Yeah. Yeah. For the most part. Just banged up, really. I was wearing my seatbelt. But the doctor put me on a bunch of medication and I can't...I can't...raise-my-arms-above-my-shoulders," he said in a rush.

"No!" Her uncle had been placed under the same restriction just after his heart surgery. "Bret! That sounds serious. That sounds like your heart."

There was a pause on the other end of the line. "Yeah," he said quietly. "It could be my heart. Anyhow," he continued, "I was thinking...all that sun, all that sand and no one to help me with my suntan lotion. A guy could get burned!"

She thought about Bret—his warm, dark complexion—and decided that was unlikely. "What about Cheryl?"

"Cheryl was months ago, Callie."

"What about whoever replaced Cheryl," she laughed stubbornly.

She thought she heard him wince. "I thought it would be more fun to make this trip with a friend."

"On a romantic Valentine's weekend!?"

"Yeah."

"Take Scott then," she said, referring to her twin brother.

"On a romantic Valentine's weekend?" he threw back with a laugh. "Scott applying my suntan lotion? That doesn't work for me. Come on, Callie. I've been online and seen a picture of the cottage. There are two *huge* beds. There's at least two feet between them. So what do you say, sweetheart?" He was giving her his best persuasive tones.

"Errm."

"Thanks, Callie. You're a good sport. There'll be an e-ticket waiting for you at Dallas Airport. My flight from Boston lands an hour before yours… I love you, Callie."

"I love you, too."

* * * * *

Callie didn't realize they'd be landing at the same concourse and that Bret would be waiting for her when she stepped through the gate. His head was turning toward her as she found him with her eyes. She hadn't seen him in almost a year and she'd forgotten what a beautiful man he was. Well, not forgotten, exactly—but it was nice to be reminded just the same.

Bret was all strong, definite, straight lines. His lower lip a generous rectangle. His fine nose was straight without any deviation. His jaw line angled out to encompass his mouth then narrowed back into a square chin. Even his eyes were clipped off polygons and the eyebrows were level, except for where they dropped off at the ends. His brown hair was straight.

Plain old brown hair. Plain old brown eyes. Put together perfectly.

Her brother Scott's best friend, Bret had been around as far back as she could remember. They'd grown up together on the same street, attended the same junior high then high school together. Played opposite each other in the winter musical their senior year. The play had ended in a kiss, and she'd thrown herself into the part, into the kiss—all fourteen times—through ten dress rehearsals and four performances.

He'd actually asked her to the Valentine's Dance that year but she'd turned him down with a laugh. He couldn't be serious!

He'd taken Mindy Walters to that dance, Jenny Rosen to the prom. Tall with big hands and long fingers, he'd led the football team to the state championship that year. She'd watched him voted in class president in the fall and crowned Prom King that spring. He'd found her in the crowd, rolled his eyes, made a face and grinned at her. Bret was like that—popularity wasn't important to him. He thought people were important and treated them that way. He made you feel special, made everyone feel special. That's one of the reasons he was so popular.

When she reached him, he leaned over to brush his lips at the side of her mouth. "Thanks for coming, sweetheart. You're a sight for sore eyes."

Taking her bag, he caught up her hand as they headed down the concourse together. She'd driven to the airport straight from work and her heels clicked as she and Bret followed the exit signs through the airport. She couldn't help a self-conscious grin when an elegant blonde turned to watch them pass, surprise stamped on her face. The woman probably wondered how someone like her could be with a man like Bret. The poor girl couldn't possibly know the handholding was purely platonic. As if Bret would settle for a size fourteen. Plain size fourteen, for that matter. Bret could do better than that. Way better than that.

"More like a sight to make your eyes sore. You didn't tell me the accident had affected your eyesight."

"There's nothing wrong with my eyes, Callie."

"Tell that to the gorgeous blonde we just passed."

"I didn't see any—"

"My point, exactly."

He gave her a grudging laugh. "Well, you look good to me."

"You've *got* to get out more."

Reaching up to wrench at his tie, Bret shook his head as he watched Callie laugh. That laugh was one of the things he loved about her—and one of the things that drove him crazy. It was a real laugh. Her laughter, her amusement, could never be mistaken for conditioned response or polite recognition. She had a real laugh and he loved it. But at the same time, it made him nuts. Because every time he tried to tell her what he thought of her, she laughed it off. Made some joke and laughed it off.

He'd seen the blonde. He just didn't think she was gorgeous. A long, thin spike of a woman as stiff as a freaking coat tree. With a cool look to chill the warmth right out of a man. How could Callie compare herself to that? Callie was all warmth—zesty, Mediterranean-style warmth. Warmth that brought everything male within him to a head. Privately, he smiled. Appropriate metaphor, considering his body's present state of response to Callie's presence.

How could Richard have let her get away? The guy had it made. Didn't deserve her but had it made. How could she have settled for someone like Richard in the first place—but that was years ago.

He was on the dimple side of her. On the left side of her face, Callie had a neat little apostrophe that accented her smile. God. How often had he fantasized about being on the other side of that dimple, his tongue in her mouth, his hands full of her—he wondered how much of her breasts he could fit in his hands and how much would be left over once they were full. How could she be so self-deprecating? Did she have no idea, whatsoever, how sexy she was? The woman was just one luscious curve after another as she walked, hips swinging, down the concourse.

Cherry lifesavers. She had lips like cherry lifesavers—red, juicy and tart. He'd been thinking about cherry lifesavers since…twelfth grade he realized—the winter musical. Cherry lifesavers, fourteen to a roll. Her black eyes were nonstop passion, full of the snap and sparkle that was—ineffably—Callie. And her hair! He watched the black curls bounce in time to her swinging gait. He imagined Callie's wild, curling hair spread out on a white pillow. Imagined gazing down on that pillow. Imagined Callie soft beneath him where other women were hard. Imagined Callie's body touching him everywhere without leaving any gaps. There'd be no gaps, save one, to fill with Callie. And the only thing hard would be his cock, filling that gap.

Bret shifted Callie's bag in front of him. His loose khaki slacks would probably hide a little indiscretion but Bret didn't have a little indiscretion at the best of times. And right now, it felt like the worst of times for his cock—it was being indiscreet in a big way.

He reached for the door that led outside and watched her through. "Thanks for coming, Callie. It means a lot to me."

Now if he could just make her understand exactly what it meant.

Chapter Two

ꟸ

As Bret signed for the rental car, Callie sneaked a look at the man beside her. His brown hair had grown a little longer than was fashionable, giving him a slightly reckless, rebel carriage. His hard, chiseled features were filled with quiet, male confidence while his eyes spilled boyish mischief.

But there was nothing remotely boyish about his body, she thought as she knelt behind him later that afternoon, doing the honors on his shoulders. She lounged on a perfect white beach, beneath a perfect blue sky, with a perfect god of a man. Squeezing more lotion into her hand, she watched him as he closed his eyes and tilted his brown face into the sun.

Ineffectually, the ocean hurried back and forth, dragging the sand beach into a slick running surface. Further out, beyond the surf, the sea was azure, and indigo, and cobalt blue, tossed together with flecks of white.

"Mmmm, that feels good," he almost purred but with more of a rumble. "Don't stop."

After kneading his shoulders until her fingers grew weary, she flopped onto the towel spread out beside him.

"Glad I brought you along," he murmured. Dropping back on his towel, he very efficiently went to sleep.

Just like a man, she thought, and took the opportunity to allow her eyes to travel the length of his long, lean body, his muscles bunched in all the right places. She couldn't find one inch of him that wasn't pure, hard male. She couldn't identify one inch of him that didn't appeal to the woman in her. On top of all that, there were several inches...but the friend in her put that thought away.

She tore her eyes from his green swim shorts and primly returned them to his—desperately she searched for a place to put her eyes that didn't elicit an illicit response from her body. Finally, she settled on his face and tugged her turquoise wrap to cover the tops of her legs.

After trying on at least twenty swimsuits, she'd settled on the colorful one-piece. It had a long, deep décolletage with a slashing diagonal pattern that wrapped her in tropical color. In the dressing room it had looked good enough that she'd reached for her brush and pulled it through her thick black curls. After adding the filmy wrap and tying it off at the hip, she was sold. The suit was expensive but worth the price of a little confidence.

She didn't know how long she lay watching him but it must have been a while. He lifted his fingers off the sand far enough to snap them. "More lotion, sweetheart."

"Slave driver," she complained, but didn't really mind.

"There ain't no free lunch," he pointed out lazily.

She watched her pale, golden hand on his brown body as she spread lotion on his chest, squirted some more in her hand and went to work on the tightly bunched muscles leading to his stomach. She laughed when he pulled his swim shorts low on his belly—dangerously low.

"You're not done, yet," he teased her.

She twisted the cap onto the plastic bottle. "I refuse to stoop that low," she said, laughing.

He shook his head slightly, eyes still closed. "I wouldn't make you stoop, Callie. Do it on your knees, darling."

The bottle of lotion landed on his chest with a smacking wallop and he curled up into a sitting position. Shaking the hair out of his eyes, he laughed at her. "That's okay, it's my turn anyway." Squeezing some of the lotion into his hand, he rubbed his hands together and got on his knees.

"I can do my own lotioning," she said, just a tick nervous. "There's nothing wrong with *my* heart."

"No? We'll see about that."

He put a finger on the end of her nose then smoothed his thumbs over her cheekbones, all of which would have been fine if he hadn't lingered so long, with his fingers holding her face. His eyes, which should have been laughing—weren't—and she found it disconcerting. She forced a laugh. "You going to take all day? My shoulders will be fried by the time you're done with my nose."

He smiled slowly as he renewed his supply of lotion. Awkwardly, he reached across her, got a hand on her shoulder then casually placed one of his knees between her legs. Now apparently comfortable, he smoothed his hands over her shoulders, up to her neck.

Callie, on the other hand, was starting to get moderately uncomfortable as he repositioned his knee, the hard warm muscles above his knee meeting the soft warm muscles between her legs. She was so distracted, she didn't realize the knuckles of his hand were inside the top of her bathing suit, traveling across her mounded breasts, edging into her full cleavage. Didn't realize it until the two erogenous zones suddenly communicated with each other with a startling amount of static.

Slapping one of his hands away, she grabbed the lotion out of his other hand. "I'll get that," she remonstrated.

"But I was just getting started."

Just getting started getting me started, she thought. "Yeah. And where exactly did you plan to end up?"

He put his eyes on her cleavage.

"Don't go there," she lectured. "A man could lose a hand down in there."

He leaned back on his heels and laughed. "I can't believe you let me get away with that." He shook his head at her and his eyes danced. "Where were you? What were you thinking?"

She looked at him, startled. Like she could tell him! "If I told you, you'd laugh," she informed him tartly.

For an instant, she was afraid he could read her mind, as he cocked an eyebrow her way. "Why don't you tell me and we'll see," he said with a soft smile. "Because I don't think I'd be laughing."

She gave him a shove but he captured one of her hands and kept it. With a soft bed of sand beneath her and the ocean's whispered lullaby in her ears, she fell asleep. When she woke, her hand was beneath Bret's hand on his belly, tucked about one inch into the top of his green swim shorts.

* * * * *

Bret left the bathroom door open and Callie watched him step into the shower with his swim shorts on. She had showered with her suit on as well. Without a washing machine, it was the most expedient way to get it clean. With a nervous glance at the bathroom door, she peeled off her suit and pulled a pink cotton dress over her head.

The beachside cabin was comfortable and quaint, and that was a relief. She was never comfortable with ostentation. The large, airy room was decorated simply in pale pinks and spring greens. In addition to two beds, there were two comfortable upholstered chairs, a couch of the same fabric and a low table. The television was inside a closed cabinet and didn't intrude to disturb the room's relaxed ambiance.

She was rummaging in her luggage for a pair of panties when Bret called her. "Do me a favor, Callie?"

"What," she called back, continuing her search.

"Help me with my hair?"

"In a minute."

"Never mind, sweetheart, I'll manage," he delivered in a pained tone that suggested he wouldn't manage very well at all.

She gave up on underwear for the moment. Stepping into the bathroom, she pulled back the shower curtain a fraction.

"Come on in, the water's fine."

His green swim shorts were on the floor of the tub and he stood with his back to her as water ran down the stacked muscles on his broad back, over his hard, square butt, and down the long, thick muscles of his legs.

"I'll…I'll get wet," she protested faintly, her eyes stuck on his perfect square butt.

He moved back a bit to take the spray on his chest. Reaching behind him, he handed her the shampoo. "Thanks, Callie. You're a good sport."

She nodded. She *was* a good sport, she thought, as she stepped into the bathtub. Anyone else might have taken Bret seriously. Might have thought all the flirting, over all the years, was real. Bret was a tease—always had been. Like this afternoon on the beach. Sneaking his hand into her bathing suit when she wasn't paying attention! She ignored the tingle that accompanied the memory and shook her head. What a nut!

As she dug her fingernails into his lathered scalp, he made all sorts of warm, growling sounds of pleasure that she had to assume were gross exaggerations. But they made her smile, nonetheless, and the truth was she spent longer washing his hair than she'd intended then helped him rinse out the soap.

"Can you get my shoulders while you're back there?"

Her black hair, now damp, twisted into curls around her face. Steamy moisture clung to her upper lip and she reached for the soap. Starting at the top of Bret's shoulders, she slowly worked her way down his back.

"Thanks," he said eventually, his voice warm and muted. "I'll take it from there."

His words brought her back to reality and she stared at her hands, low on his flanks, moving slowly on either side of his butt. With a start, she pulled her hands away.

"Maybe you could help me with something else," he said softly, and turned to face her.

Her eyes widened as she stared down at his full-out hard-on.

Chapter Three

ꟿ

Callie took an abrupt step backward in the tub. "Where did that come from?"

Bret grimaced, but whether it was from disappointment or embarrassment wasn't apparent. "I don't know. I'm thinking maybe it's the medication I'm on."

"Really! Because that doesn't look like the result of muscle relaxants," she pointed out with a laugh.

He didn't laugh. "I don't know what they've got me on, but something's driving me crazy." One slow, sliding step and he had her pinned against the wall beneath his wet body. His warm, wet lips were slippery on her mouth then on her neck as he rubbed his erection into her rise. "Pink," he mumbled into her neck.

"Bret!" Her voice was full of shocked refusal.

"Oh God, Callie. Why did it have to be pink? Help me," he breathed into her ear. "I...won't come inside you. Just let me rub myself out on your...against your body," he managed with great difficulty. "I'm so hot, it will only take a minute, I promise."

The shower continued to pound down behind them while Callie's blood pounded in counterpoint. She was wet and warm, revise that—hot—everywhere his naked skin touched her, wet in one place he hadn't touched her and damp just about everywhere else.

As he continued to grind against the rise of her crotch, she gritted her teeth and canted her hips forward in an unauthorized attempt to align her cleft with the thick ridge of his erection. She got a piece of him between her lips and her sex throbbed to life as her body cried out for a bigger piece.

He stopped suddenly and stared into her eyes. "God help me."

He took her hand and wrapped it around his shaft then pumped out onto the skirt of her dress.

She felt his cock expand in her hand, hard and thick inside stretched skin, just before he shot. The slug of male warmth hit her groin and she gasped as he kept coming onto her dress in hot surges. She stared down at his ejaculate as it dripped a shining path down the front of her skirt. Saw her hand still wrapped around the base of his cock.

Her fingers sprang open to release him.

"Shit," he said, still holding onto her. His expression was surprised as he looked down between their bodies. "Shit, I've made a mess. I'm sorry, Callie." Without consultation, he turned her around him in the shower and moved her under the warm pounding water. With the thin pink dress sucking up to her every curve, he stood behind her and ran his hands down the front of her dress. "Shit," he continued to say the whole time.

Soaping his hands, he lathered her breasts slowly with spread fingers before he moved his hands down over her belly and into her loins. His actions were slow and thorough—and probably methodical—she thought. So why did it feel so damn intimate?

Feeling warm and melty, she closed her eyes and leaned her back against his chest as he continued to stroke his spread fingers slowly over the wet pink cotton, down her belly, down the front of her thighs. When the width of his thumb stroked down over her mons, it prompted a stunning reaction between her legs as her groin filled with sparking heat. And when his fingers smoothed back upward over the same route, all those sparks converged at once into a pyrotechnic response of brilliant proportions—a reaction that would have required lead sunglasses to view.

Abruptly he twisted the faucet, stepped out of the tub and threw her a towel as he wrapped another around his waist. But not before she saw he was erect again. "Are you okay?" she asked him.

He ran a hand into his hair. "Yeah, Callie. Damn. I'm sorry, but I could use a drink. I know a place on the beach."

She'd only just toweled off the dripping wet when he pulled her out the cottage door and across the sand. "I'm still wet," she protested.

He stopped to study her. The breeze whipped at his khaki slacks and the thin, beige canvas sucked at his legs. "Yes, you are," he said. "You look good that way. I love you all pink and wet. Don't ever change."

She laughed as he reached an arm around her shoulders and led her down the beach.

Chapter Four

ꟸ

With his elbow on the table and his chin in his hand, Bret smiled at Callie as she ordered a drink in a tall glass, her selection based primarily on the colorful picture propped on the table. She caught his eye and wriggled a bit under his gaze. Then wriggled some more, trying to cool her hot lips on the cool vinyl seat. Bret's body was snugged up close to hers. Too close for comfort—she suppressed a shiver. But not quite close enough for actual full-out copulation.

The long thin stretch of restaurant was comfortably lit, shadowed but not dark. The interior was flamboyantly decorated in colorful fifties vinyl, sparkling Formica and shining chrome.

"Here's to beautiful women," Bret said when the drinks were delivered and raised his short glass to clink against her tall one.

She snorted. "Yeah. Too bad you didn't bring one with you."

His smile flattened out into a line. "To old friends, then. Who are always there for you."

He moved his hand to pull at one of her damp tendrils and she realized she probably looked a mess. Excusing herself, she wobbled over to the door marked "ladies". Standing before the mirror, she pushed her hair around and stared at her flushed cheeks, her dilated pupils. She frowned a painful look of sympathy for the woman in the mirror. God, she had it bad—had it bad for an old friend who was flash enough to date movie stars. While she! She!

Critically, she appraised her reflection.

Well, her hair wasn't bad, really. It was probably her best feature, full of wild, generous abandon. The black curls weren't too bad against her warm, gold skin, especially with her cheeks pinked up the way they were now. With blue eyes, instead of black, she might have been attractive…maybe…if she dropped about twenty pounds.

Her shoulders sagged a bit but she forced them back bravely before she opened the restroom door and made her way back to their table. Smiling brightly, she approached the table and watched Bret's eyes as they followed her all the way back. For a few seconds, she allowed herself the fantasy that she was a ravishing beauty and Bret watched her with ravishing intent, devouring her with his eyes.

He was on his feet, waiting for her when she reached the table.

Together, they dropped onto the bench seat. "I'm sorry," he said as she started with a jump. Slowly, he dragged his hand from beneath her bottom.

"I'm sorry too," she said, her cheeks shading from pink to deep rose. Yeah, she was sorry all right. Sorry he'd removed his hand.

His expression solemn, Bret stirred his drink with a finger. "But you *are* beautiful, Callie," he said, as though she'd never left.

She laughed. "Compared to what?"

"Compared to anything," he told her quietly. "And everything."

"You haven't seen everything."

"I like what I see, now."

"And *that's* only because you haven't seen everything. You haven't seen the parts that wobble," she laughed.

"Perhaps you should show me then." He watched her face until she averted her eyes then let his eyes slip down her dress to her breasts.

She followed his gaze to her erect nipples threatening the thin cotton stretched tight across her chest.

He cocked his head. "Happy to see me?" he guessed. He raised his eyes from her nipples back to her face.

Quickly, she shook her head. "It's just a bit chilly in here. The dress is still wet."

He nodded and snuggled his body up closer to hers, curling an arm around her waist. "Is that better?" he breathed against her neck.

She shivered.

"I'm sorry. You really are cold, aren't you? I should have given you time to change. Here." Picking her up at the waist, he moved her onto his lap and rubbed his hands down her arms.

This isn't helping, she thought, as she shivered again. Hand clenched around the base of her glass, she sipped her drink while Bret, fingers spread, rubbed her thighs. His warm proximity started a thrum between her legs that was so strong she was afraid he'd feel her hot pulse in his lap. Distracted, she didn't notice the skirt of her dress moving incrementally upward with every stroke of his hand. Didn't notice until he was stroking his hand over the smooth, bare skin of her thighs. She gave him a look of dismay and he returned a hooded smile.

He looked down at her thighs, exposed under his hand, hidden behind the table. "I think I have you warmed up now."

Understatement of the year, she thought weakly. She was warmed up all right. She was ready to go thermonuclear.

Withdrawing his hand, Bret's cheek brushed her chest as he motioned the waiter for a second round of drinks and the hard tips of her breasts responded with an aching demand for additional contact. She almost jumped when his hand returned to circle her knee. He talked about his work for a while but she was barely cognizant of the topic as he continued to stroke her thighs absentmindedly, each stroke bringing his hand minutely closer to her sex.

He stopped suddenly. "You seem tense, Callie. Is everything all right?" His voice was rich and soft, and deep.

Eyes glassy, she nodded and felt his hand as is slipped between her thighs, his index finger moving downward to feather along the outside of her swollen labia. She ended the nod with a sudden intake of breath that must have traveled across the restaurant and possibly the island.

Bret looked up at her from beneath dark lashes. "You're not wearing panties," he murmured.

She struggled to laugh and shook her head. "You rushed me out of the room before I had a chance!"

He gave her a disappointed smile. "And there I was hoping you'd planned it. For me. I'm sorry," he said in a quiet, flat voice, "but at least you're finally warm." Angling his hand slightly, he pulled his finger up through the length of her damp pussy.

Her breath whined in through her teeth.

"Hot, actually. And wet. But that's not for me, either, is it? Don't disappoint me, Callie. Tell me you're not hot for me."

She hesitated, caught in his smoldering gaze. He slid his finger back and forth at the top of her cleft. "Go ahead, Callie. Tell me it's not me."

"Bret," she said with great difficulty, "I don't want this to happen."

His finger stopped and he nodded, removed his finger from her hot rutted sex to stir his drink thoughtfully. She watched the ice go around in the glass, watched his finger go around in the glass. She closed her eyes and didn't see his hand drop behind the table again. But she felt it. Felt his finger ice-cold and firm against her burning clit. She gasped and he let her, disregarding the bartender's glance from across the restaurant, certain that the table hid his actions.

She watched his hand longingly when he returned his finger to stir into the drink again. "All right," he said, "as long as you don't want this, I'll see what I can do to cool you off." He pulled an ice cube out of his drink and hefted it thoughtfully for a moment before he returned to the glass.

This time she watched when his hand dropped beneath the table and his finger nudged against her swollen lips. She opened her legs to allow his finger's intrusion and he pushed into her lips. His cold finger dragged back over her clit where it remained to tease her with a light touch and random movement. Without warning, a whole handful of cold fingers intruded to widen her and stroke at her throbbing sex with regularity she could set her clock by. And she knew she was about two strokes away from orgasm.

Leaning her head against his, she moaned. "Bret. I think we'd better leave."

"We will, angel," he whispered into her neck. "Just as soon as I'm finished here."

When the waiter dragged past with two patrons in his wake, Bret moved his hand back up to his drink.

In that instant, Callie was off his lap and out the door.

Chapter Five

ꕥ

Standing swiftly, eyes on the door, Bret pulled his wallet out and threw some bills on the table then followed.

He found Callie, waist-deep in the surf. "I love you," he yelled into the waves.

"There's an original line."

"I do, Callie."

She sloshed toward him. "Bret. If you want to have sex with me…"

"Of course I want to have sex with you. Because you're beautiful, funny, generous but most importantly because—and you'd better listen to this part—because I love you." He watched the wet skirt of her dress as the ocean sucked it up around her curves. "I want to get my arms around you and—"

"I'm not sure that's physically possible," she laughed. "Just how long are your arms?"

"Come here and I'll show you."

But she turned and waded through the surf, sandals dangling in the hand at her side. He paralleled her route, ten feet of flighty, indecisive water separating them as they made their way down the beach and back toward the cabin.

"Don't make me come in after you."

She shook her head. "Don't, Bret. Don't do this to me. And don't say you love me again. Yes, we love each other—as friends. But I don't see how it could ever be anything more."

Funny how it sounded more like a question to him than a statement—and a pleading question, at that. His eyes narrowed, lit with frustration. "Well," he muttered, "I was willing to demonstrate…but I guess you don't want that, do you, Callie?"

Head down, hands shoved in his pockets, he turned and slanted across the sand away from the surf.

Callie winced and turned out a full circle in the water. Slowly, she moped her way across the beach after Bret.

Hesitating before the cabin door, she took a deep breath. When she opened the door, she found the room filled with flowers. Pink and red, peach gladioli. Where did you find gladioli in February? Someone had emptied a bucket of rose petals on the floor. She looked up from the carpet of pink. "Part of the package?" she asked him, closing the door behind her.

"Not exactly." He was loosening the final button on his shirt. She watched him rip the shirt off, ball it up and fling it at the floor. "Tell me you don't want me, Callie."

Her eyes followed his hands up, as his wrist twisted in front of his crotch then appeared to drag up along his fly. She watched his fingers reach for the button at his waist. Groaning, she turned away from him, standing in the middle of the room. "It would never work, Bret. For me. I couldn't just…just have sex with you and…and leave it at that…"

"Neither could I," he interjected.

"…not without a broken heart."

"Callie."

"Look at you, Bret. And look at me," she laughed as she turned back to him, hands outstretched in demonstration. "You could have any woman you wanted."

"Yeah, I know. I've had them. All of them, it feels like. I don't want them. I want you."

"When you walk through airports, women turn around and stare. Look at me! I'm…not exactly centerfold stuff."

He looked a little guilty.

"You've had centerfold stuff?"

"She wasn't like you," he said soberly. "She had *no* sense of humor."

"Who worries about humor at a time like that?"

"Nobody. But it's nice to have a little before. And after." He gave her a wry grin. "I only pretended to forget her name."

Callie's jaw dropped. "You pretended to forget Miss October's name?"

"January."

"What?"

"Miss January," he corrected her. "You would have known I was kidding."

"You're a tease."

"And you're beautiful."

"I'm no Miss January, Bret."

He shook his head. "No. You're no Miss January. But I don't want Miss January. I'm ready for Miss February. I want *you*, Callie."

She laughed, unconvincingly. "Then you want a lot, Bret."

"Yeah, I want a lot." But he didn't return her smile. Instead, he dropped into a chair and regarded her with impatience. "That's it. Keep laughing, Callie. You always have a comeback, don't you?" He sighed and raised his eyes to the ceiling. "Well let's hear your comeback to this, Callie. Have you ever been French kissed—"

"Yes, of course—"

" —between your legs?"

Her nostrils flared and, for once, she was silent.

"Because that's the way I want to kiss you. I want you kneeling on the floor, with your skirt shoved up to your waist. I want to pull your legs apart. *I* want to. I want to put my head between your legs and put a long French kiss into your sex, lick at your sweet, pink folds until you come into my mouth."

He put his eyes on hers.

"I want you pinned against the wall, my cock all the way in, my hands spread in a hopeless attempt to contain your breasts, loving your breasts, feeling your body strain for mine while my hips are coming at you, hard.

"I want you on your hands and knees, on the bed, while I stand behind you. Your dress pushed up over your hips, your panties pulled down and stretching across your thighs. I want to see your pussy, thick and swollen, between pink dress and black panties, want to cup you in my hand, stroke you with my lips. I want to get my cock between your legs and push it through your folds until you're wet enough to coat me. See your slit wet for me. Hear you panting for me. I want to pull your cheeks apart—*I* want to—then drive into you. I want to fill you with my cock, watch you on my cock when you start to come."

The room was silent. His legs spread casually as he slouched in the chair and he drew his wrist up the front of his pants, up the length of his erection. "I want you on your knees in front of me, between my legs as I sit in this chair. I want to run my fingers into your hair while your head is buried in my lap. I want to feel your lips warm on my sex, sucking on my cock as your fingers reach for my balls.

"Do I have your attention, Callie?

"Because there's one thing more I want, even more than all of this. I want you to marry me."

Chapter Six

ഌ

Shocked into silence, Callie dropped to her knees on the petalled carpet. Without purpose, she started collecting the bits of pink as she attempted to collect her runaway feelings.

Bret got to his feet and dropped to his knees in front of her. "I love you, Callie. Why do you find that so hard to believe?"

She turned her head.

"I want you, Callie. I want *you*. You've been pushing me away for years and I'm tired of it."

Dropping back on her heels, she pulled away from him.

"You're beautiful," he whispered.

She pressed her lips together and shook her head.

"Damn it, Callie. Would it kill you to accept a compliment for a change?"

She shook her head again. "It would probably just give me heartburn."

"Let me try this again. I'll tell you you're beautiful. And you say…"

She gave him a stubborn look.

"Thank you! You say thank you!"

"Thank you," she said obediently. "That's a very kind lie."

He smiled at her reluctantly. "You're hopeless. What did you say to Richard when he complimented you?"

She averted her eyes.

"How did you answer Richard when he said you were beautiful?"

Uninvited, unwelcome tears came out of nowhere and blindsided her.

"God, Callie. I'm sorry. I'm sorry, darling." He got a hand behind her neck and pulled her toward him.

"It's not your fault," she sobbed into his chest. "It's not your fault he never…"

Bret smothered her into his chest. "What a dick," he said harshly. He shook his head while she shook in his arms.

Pulling her face out of his shirt, he smoothed her tears away with his thumbs. His lips gravitated toward hers in one of those slow, breath-holding approaches. Finally, they touched down on hers. She found herself with her neck arched, her head back, as she sucked up as much of that kiss as she could fit in her mouth.

Getting his hand under her skirt, he ran his hand between her legs. "Do me a favor," he murmured into her mouth.

"No," she protested faintly. "No. Bret. I'm done doing you favors."

But his tongue was already in her mouth, distracting her while his fingers worked to release the buttons that held the cotton tight across her breasts. Ineffectually, her fingers fought with his. Eventually giving up, her fingers followed his, doing up the work he'd undone.

In a burst of impatience, he grasped her wrists. "You're going to listen to me, Callie." His eyes searched the room and found the tie he'd discarded earlier, straggled and twisted at the edge of the bed. Snatching it up, he wrapped it around her wrists then decided her arms were in the way and changed his mind. Pulling her arms behind her, he rewrapped her wrists. "You're beautiful, Callie."

"No, you're beautiful, Bret."

He stopped and smiled at her. "You think so?"

As she struggled to get her feet beneath her, he looked around for inspiration. With desperate ingenuity aided by superior male strength, he reached for the corner of the bed, pulled it up an inch, whipped the end of his tie under the leg of the heavy bed and dropped it again.

Callie stared at him, appalled. Her wrists were tied behind her and secured at the floor by twelve inches of striped power-tie.

Chapter Seven

ꕥ

Callie tugged on the tie, wide eyes searching his for explanation.

"You're going to listen to me, Callie," Bret said as he loosened her buttons, picking them off one-by-one from the top down. "I don't know. Maybe if I were bald—skinny—had a big nose, I'd feel like I needed a...Barbie doll on my arm. But I need you."

"Bret."

"Tell me you don't love me, Callie." Working his way down through her buttons, he stooped to press a wet tongue against the cotton covering one nipple. Pulling back, he viewed her breast with dissatisfaction. Scratching a fingernail over the wet cotton that covered her nipple, he repeated the action until his persistence was rewarded and her nipple wasn't flat anymore. "And while you're at it, tell your two friends here."

Smiling slightly, he lowered his mouth to suck on the cotton hiding her second nipple, pulling at it with his teeth. He leaned back to survey the result. Both nipples stood erect beneath the wet cotton in proud, showy, prominent display. He smiled completely. "Tell me you don't want me," he whispered and raised his eyes to hers.

She looked like she was going to cry. "You're too good for me."

All but done with her buttons, he pulled the skirt of her dress to her waist and tied it in a knot. "Oh God, Callie. Just give me a chance and I'll show you how good I can be for you." He rested his hands on the tops of her thighs and leaned his lips into hers, relieved when she neither laughed nor pulled away. Pressing his advantage, he angled his lips on hers, encouraged her lips open and stroked his tongue into her mouth, finally got his tongue on the inside of that dimple and groaned with the kind of satisfaction that only comes after years of anticipation. At the same time, he got his knees inside hers and pushed her legs open while both his hands went behind her to pull her lower body toward him. He tugged the round cheeks of her behind apart and slid his fingers deep into the saddle between her cheeks. They both caught up a gasp as his fingers intruded into slick, wet territory. Ending the kiss abruptly, they stared at each other. "Oh God, Callie, tell me all that moisture's for me."

She pulled away from him, but her eyes were dark and her breathing was rampant enough to pop the final button holding her heavy breasts within the bodice of her dress. When her breasts fell out of their cotton enclosure, she stared down at them in dismay. Then up at him in shock. Because Bret groaned as he brought his hands around to cage her breasts. She watched his hands rotate around the warm curves of her breasts.

"Look at these hands, Callie. These have got to be size D hands."

"Double D," she squeaked.

His eyes joined his hands as he worshiped her breasts. "We're a perfect fit. I've had thin little bits of women, Callie. I want more…not a lot more," he said quickly, "just a bit more. I want a woman with breasts that spill out of my hands, a woman deep enough to take all of me, a woman with enough love to surround me and I want something to hold on to when I'm loving her."

She laughed, but it was weak. "Well, I have more than enough, Bret."

His face was serious. "Don't laugh me off, Callie. You've been laughing me off since junior high. It isn't funny anymore." He covered her mouth with his and moved his hand between her legs. His finger was cool on her hot sex as it gently plowed her furrow open from the top of her cleft to her warm, wet opening. Dipping three fingers into her well, he dragged his wet fingers back up her pussy again. She shuddered into his mouth. He stopped kissing her and searched her eyes. "Tell me you don't want me, Callie."

She closed her eyes.

She felt him move away, felt him pull her legs further apart. She didn't fight it. His longish hair was against the inside of her thighs as he slid his head between her legs and, with his hands high on the inside of her thighs, pushed her legs wider, pulling her pussy down to meet his lips. Sexual tension had been building in her all day. Hours of heated, ramping expectation had her sex fully primed and ready for orgasm—she didn't keep him waiting. He gave her a long, slow French kiss and she came into his mouth.

Her head went back and her body was a wave that fed into his mouth. His tongue continued its soft stroking action along her sensitive fleshy folds and into her opening while she quaked through a long series of contractions, her orgasm strung out to indecent length under the action of his unrelenting, probing tongue.

She was crying by the time he got to his knees again. "I love you," she sobbed. "I've always loved you. I can't remember when I didn't."

He pulled her against his chest. "I know. I know, Callie." With a brutal yank, the tie was free and he fumbled to loosen the knot that held her wrists. He held her tightly while his heart raced. His heart, like his penis long neglected, felt like it would burst. But he continued to hold her until her sobbing subsided into the occasional shudder. Pulling her chin up, he thumbed the tears from below her eyes.

She shrugged apologetically. "Well, you wanted moisture," she told him. "I hope you're satisfied."

He shook his head. "As a matter of fact…" he grimaced as he glanced down in the direction of his cock. "Do me a favor?" he said softly.

She smiled up at him and nodded.

With the outlook of release on the horizon, Bret's passion surfaced with a vengeance. Picking her up, he swung her onto the bed and got his hand inside her dress. With a handful of cotton bunched in his fist, he wrenched at the pink stuff that concealed her body—the dress that stood between him and everything he must have next. The pink cotton gave as he ripped downward. Tattered shreds of cotton teased her nipples into taut buds as he shoved the remnants out of his way to expose her body.

He took a breath and held it as his eyes ate up every round inch of her.

For just an instant, his hand hovered above her chest before the rough heel of his palm scraped down between her breasts. He watched his own hand's progress as it headed into the curling hair between her legs. Her pelvis canted upward as her head went back and his hand was filled with warm, wet pussy. With his open hand, he worked her lips apart until he could get all his fingers between them—flat against her sex spread beneath his hand—and stroked at her slick, wet labia. Thumbed her clitoris until she gasped through gritted teeth; then left his thumb to trouble her clit while he thrust two fingers into her vagina. Her bottom came up off the bed at least four inches as her body tried to receive him, tried to take in more of him.

"That's it, Callie," he whispered. "Reach for me, sweetheart."

With his left hand, he fumbled to loosen the button of his slacks, groaning when it resisted. His cock was desperate to get out and get on her. As his fingers struggled with the button, the edge of his hand rasped impatiently at his dick.

With a desperate wrench, the button popped and he rucked the pants out of his way. His hips were moving before he got between her legs, the soft, moist skin of his cock dragging at the skin of her hips then the top of her thighs. He fell on her with a hunger that had never been properly addressed during his lifetime. One arm had to be sacrificed to support his weight and he slipped it beneath her shoulder. But the other arm—the other hand—was free to live out a long-awaited fantasy that involved his large hand and her fabulous breasts.

With his right hand rounding her left breast and his lips eating hers, he thrust his hips against her and rubbed his cock into her skin—everywhere he made contact—as he made his way toward her pussy. He felt her hands move up his sides to clutch beneath his arms and pull his bare chest against the skin of her breasts. Felt her soft, warm body rock to answer the thrust of his hips. Felt the friction of her velvet skin, warm against the cock he could not still.

But he had to have more.

He had to get her on his dick.

He pulled at her knee as he pushed between her legs and felt the woman he loved spread her legs for his entry. With a growl of approval, he dragged his lower body up to meet her pussy, found her opening and with a thrust, hooked her body on his cock. Her body arched to receive him—all of him.

"Oh God, yes," he whispered into her lips. "Cherry lifesavers."

"Bret!"

His name came out of her mouth all mangled and his cock responded with a thrusting surge of angry excitement.

"Knees up, Callie. Ah, God please, darling."

When her knees came up beside him, he coaxed them higher with a firm hand then pressed them wider with a hard palm, as he thrust into her. And thrust into her. And kept thrusting at her until she came again, in wild suffering pleasure that prompted his own release. He hammered into her with an iron cock and struck her cervix until she saw sparks—kept coming at her until his cock gave up the fuck and was finally quenched, drenched in his own release.

"Oh God, love," he moaned into her mouth. "How could you keep this from me all these years?" He looked down at their bodies, sex-heated, damp and close—and stiffened inside her.

Her eyes opened slowly and gave him an uncertain look of surprise.

He returned her a small, but ruthless smile. "What do you want for lunch tomorrow?" he asked.

"Lunch? What about breakfast?"

He nodded down at her as he moved on her slowly. "I have a feeling that, by the time we're ready for breakfast, it will probably be lunchtime."

Chapter Eight

ഇ

Room service had delivered by the time Callie woke up. A little table had been set with white Irish linen, flowers, coffee and two covered plates. Wrapping the shambles of her pink dress around her, Callie padded over to the table and lifted the cover off one of the plates.

Rubbing a towel into his wet hair, Bret came through the bathroom door. She smiled at his face then all the way down his hard chest and firm belly to the front of his boxer shorts.

He leaned a kiss into her neck on the way to his chair. "Good morning, sweetheart. I ordered pancakes for you." He poured out two cups of steaming coffee while she situated her napkin in her lap. "I'll bet you're starving after last night—all the exercise," he teased. "I'm sorry. I should have bought you dinner."

She nodded at the thick stack of pancakes and peeked up at him from beneath a shield of lashes. His long, lean torso was dark against the pastel background of the room. His tight muscles shifted economically as he spread a thin sheen of butter onto a triangle of toast.

"I wasn't hungry," she told him.

Suddenly reluctant to eat in front of this perfect man, her throat constricted as a sick knot took hold of her stomach. Unreasonably, Callie found herself unwilling to add one more pound—one more centimeter—to her body, the body that Bret Haverston made love to.

Glancing up from his toast, Bret caught her stare and returned it with a slow smile. He didn't look hungry, either—

at least, not for food. His eyes continued into her cleavage as the open dress barely managed to hide her nipples.

Shyly, she fumbled the fork into her hand and cut a wedge out of the stack of cakes. Trying to appear dainty but feeling clumsy, she maneuvered the fork toward her mouth. At the last possible moment, she saw the inelegant lump sliding off her fork. She made a dive for the pancake with her other hand and only ended up looking more awkward. The torn skirt of her dress gaped open and she felt the warm pancake on her bare thighs.

Mortified, she looked up at Bret as he blurred behind a sheen of tears. Perfect, lean, graceful Bret. Eating breakfast with a size fourteen that had a pile of pancake in her lap.

Carefully, Bret lowered his knife as Callie looked down at the mess in her lap.

"Wouldn't you like some syrup with that?" he was asking.

Callie shook her head.

Suddenly, he was beside her, a small china jug in his hand, rotating her chair backward with a push.

Callie reached a knuckle up to catch a tear and ran into Bret's fingers. She felt the tear flicked away at the tip of Bret's thumb. At the same time, she felt something warm pour onto her lap and spread then trickle into the small triangle of space at the top of her legs.

Her eyes widened on his.

"Look at you," he said, holding her eyes with his warm gaze, "can't take you anywhere." Together they watched the pool of syrup as it disappeared, sinking between her legs. "Guess I'll just have to take you here."

He ate the pancake first, using his teeth, she noted, as he dragged his teeth over her flesh. Once that was accomplished, he commenced to lick up everything else he could readily reach. He ran his tongue over the tops of her thighs, easing her legs apart as he worked his way in deeper between her sticky thighs. His rough tongue stroked her skin with thorough, meticulous care as he lapped up the syrup that coated her thighs. So carefully and slowly, she thought she would lose her mind before his tongue got to the point—the point of her desire. Finally, he ran his tongue lightly over the outer lips of her labia then stopped.

"I think I got most of it," he said, and she watched his eyes resting between her legs, wanting to yank his head down and hold his mouth firmly against her pulsing pussy. "If you want me to get the rest…you're going to have to move your legs apart."

Moaning, Callie closed her eyes and Bret rose to press a sweet, sticky kiss onto her lips. At the end of the kiss, he ran his tongue around the outside of her mouth. "Open your legs, Callie, and I'll finish licking you right. I'll lick you right up to your finish. I'll lick you until you make your own syrup and it pours out on my tongue. Then I'll make you come into my mouth. Spread your legs, Callie."

Callie moaned again, shyness warring with the desire hot and ready between her legs. Reaching for his cup, Bret filled his mouth with coffee as he leaned over and slid his hand around her breast, pulling the ragged pink fabric back to expose her breast. Bending his head, he sucked one of her nipples into his warm liquid-filled mouth.

Callie gasped and her eyes opened just in time to watch Bret sprinkle a handful of sugar onto her wet nipple. When he finished sucking her other nipple, he decorated it in the same manner. Holding her breath, she stared down at the sweet, frosted confection he'd made of her nipples then smiled up at him suddenly. "They're beautiful," she said, her voice full of wonder and revelation.

He smiled and nodded as he lowered his mouth to suck at one of the sparkling mounds. "Oh God, they're beautiful," he murmured as he moved his head to her other breast. Callie's hand tightened in his hair and pulled his head onto her chest as her back arched, pushing her breast full against his mouth. Reaching to take one of her hands from his hair, he pushed it into the full round swell at the side of her chest. Together they fed her nipple into his mouth.

When Callie whimpered, Bret answered with a groaning rumble, then he was on his knees again, one of his shoulders under her left leg, as he placed her foot on the table. He kissed the curling hair above her mons and dropped his tongue into the top of her cleft. With his hand, he stroked up along the underside of her right thigh and pushed her leg wide. When he sucked up her clit, she almost jumped into his mouth. Legs spread, open and exposed, she writhed in the chair.

"Look at this ripe, luscious berry," he was saying, and Callie sucked in a sob when he returned his lips to suck again. "Pass the cream, Callie. Never mind. I'll get it." A moment later, he was tipping the point of the creamer at the top of her cleft; the cool cream on her hot clit made her legs stretch apart and her sex cant upward off the chair.

With his head between her legs, Bret's mouth was all over her sex, kissing and prodding, and sucking and eating. With a rough tongue, he thrust against her vulva several times and she came in clutching, wrenching orgasm. When her legs tried to close, he barred them open with his forearms as he stroked his tongue through the length of her wet, pink sex.

Finally, her body slackened and he stood, ready for his own release.

He pushed his shorts down to release his stiff cock. Leaning forward, he put his thick hood against her lips. "I want to see your lips on me," he rasped, and it wasn't a request.

Callie took him into her mouth as deeply as she could. She sucked out the length of his shaft then let him go. With the sugar bowl in one hand, she tipped the bowl as she pulled his shaft down to bury his cock-head in the white crystals. It came out with a proud helmet of sparkling white. Callie flicked out her tongue to swirl around his tip, then sucked gently at his first few inches. Giving him up again, she pulled away reaching for the sugar. Bret groaned and stopped her with a fist beneath her chin. Unable to wait any longer, his hand grasped her chin—the other hand was at the back of her head as he thrust his cock against her lips. "Oh God, Callie. Take me in, love. Take all of me, Callie."

With her hands on his flanks, she swallowed him as deeply as she could.

Hands braced behind her, on the back of her chair, Bret's hips jerked forward as he insinuated himself more deeply into her mouth. He drove his hips at her fiercely, helpless to stop himself.

Almost choking on his massive erection, Callie felt him expand in her mouth and thicken between her teeth. His fingers grasped at her skull as he surged and she swallowed down his come as it rushed into her throat.

* * * * *

"We should go to the beach," Callie murmured.

"We should." Bret sighed lazily and made no other move whatsoever.

"What time is it?"

Bret turned his head to the clock beside the bed. "Three."

"We slept through lunch?"

"And made love through breakfast."

She laughed. "And dinner last night."

He shook his head. "We made love through dinner-time, not dinner."

They both turned to look at the little table.

"Made love through breakfast," they said together.

He turned his head and smiled at her. "Hungry?"

"Yeah, I'm hungry," she told him. "You got anything left?"

He closed his eyes and nodded up at the ceiling. "I could probably scrape something up, with the right encouragement."

"What do you mean?"

His lips angled up at the edges. "How'd you like to help me live out a long-held fantasy?"

Chapter Nine

ꟗ

"It doesn't involve anything complicated," Bret said quickly. "Only you. And some black panties." He rolled onto his side and snugged his body up against hers. "Do you have a pair?

"There is a God," he murmured when Callie nodded. His eyes followed her as she rolled off the bed and stepped over to her suitcase.

"Shall I take the dress off?"

"No. Please. Leave the dress on."

"But it's all—"

"Perfect. It's all perfect." He rolled to sit on the bed as she pulled the black lace panties up her legs. "Do you remember that time I busted into your bedroom? We were about fifteen. Scott was chasing me. I didn't even know you were home."

Her cheeks went pink. After all these years, they went pink.

"I was dressing."

"You were wearing black bikini underpants. You were leaning over, trying to get your breasts, all of those big, full, teenage breasts into a black brassiere."

"Was it black?"

He nodded slowly. "The brassiere was black. Your panties were black." Bret stood and made his way over to her, took her hand and led her back to the bed. "It was late winter—February—but warm, and your window was open. The curtains were floating into the room. They were pink."

He turned her around to face the bed. His chest was against her back and he placed a warm kiss on the side of her neck.

"Get on the bed, Callie. On your knees, darling."

Callie knelt on the bed while Bret ran his hands down to hold the bottom of her heavy breasts. His lips were against her ear. "You know what I want, Callie. Don't make me beg."

She leaned forward onto her hands and felt Bret's hands travel down over her hips then thighs, catching at what was left of her pink skirt and pushing it up over her bottom. Her panties were next as Bret dragged them down to the top of her thighs. She felt him move away. "Bret?"

Bret leaned against the wall, a few feet from the bed. "Oh God, Callie. I've waited so long for this. Just let me enjoy it." With his hand beneath his dick, he stroked out his length. "This is what I'd see when I was a kid, pumping myself out in the shower. This was what I'd think about when I was with Miss January, every time I was with Miss January. And every other woman for that matter." With his hand wrapped around his shaft, he pumped himself slowly. His eyes moved to his stiffened cock. "Damn. I've never been this big before, Callie. And I've never wanted anything so much."

Callie stifled a moaning sob. Bret's words initiated a tingle that raced down her spine and arced into the space between her legs in probing pulsations of expectation. Her body was crying for Bret. Bret's thick, uncompromising entry. Her back wanted to arch and responding to instinct, she dropped onto her elbows and opened her legs a fraction. With her knees parted and her back curved, her heavy breasts rested on the bed.

The position she found herself in was eroticism defined and her heart pounded into the mattress. The thought of Bret, behind her, his legs spread, his hands smoothing up her legs to pull her open, caused her sex to reverberate like a drum beneath the drumstick's brutal caress. She wanted to beg for that caress, but restrained the wanton impulse.

"I'm ready, Bret," she said with a tight voice.

"I hope you are," he said, moving toward her. "Because once I get inside you, I don't think I'm going to be able to be gentle. Do you think you can take it?"

"I'll take it, Bret. All of it, I promise. I'll take it all. Now."

Bret dropped to his knees behind her, caressing the bottom he'd exposed between black lace and pink cotton. He kissed her smooth golden skin and pulled her cheeks apart. The puffy lips of her labia were as pretty as anything he'd ever seen in the best men's magazines and he couldn't help but kiss her, right there where she wanted him.

His lips on her silken flesh was a gentle offering, a tender apology for what was to follow—the brutal ravaging her pussy would receive when he shoved his cock deep in her cunt and started pounding into her.

"Bret," she cried. "I'm ready. Please, Bret."

"Just one more kiss," he said against the lips of her swollen labia.

She pushed herself backward and rubbed her sex into the kiss. "Bret," she panted, "Now. Please. Come on, Bret."

Bret stood, spread his legs, and entered her hard and all the way. His hands on her hips locked her bottom tight against his groin. Callie screamed and he stopped there, in her as far as he could go. "Are you okay?" His voice was raw and hoarse.

"There's…there's just so much of you. Give me a minute…to adjust."

He pulled his cock back several inches and looked down at the thick root of his glistening shaft. "I can't wait," he said.

And started slamming into her.

"Oh—my—God—Bret!" she cried in time with his first four thrusts. Her body was primed for his pumping action and her mind pushed her the remaining short distance toward orgasm as she shared this patently carnal act with the man she loved. "Come on, Bret," she whispered as she started to come. "Come on." Then she was screaming the same words.

Bret's hips pistoned at a savage pace, the bottom of his shaft scraping over the elastic edge of her panties, his balls swinging up to hit the fence of stretched black lace. There was a tearing sound as the lace frayed then his balls were up against Callie and all her warmth. He didn't come until she stopped screaming.

*****

When Callie came out of the shower, the table had been cleared except for an envelope with her name on it. A thick, creamy envelope with a rough textured surface and pink undertones. Staring across the room at it, Callie tied her bright, silk robe closed. She opened it expecting to find a Valentine. With a small frown, she shuffled through the little pile of travel itineraries and receipts. Going back to the itineraries, she checked the dates. They were issued the day he'd called her.

Bret watched her from across the room, a towel around his neck.

"There was no free trip?"

He shook his head.

Her eyes were on the floor, on the curling petals, as she nodded her head.

"I wasn't in a car accident," he told her. "There's nothing wrong with me and I'm not on any medication."

"There's nothing wrong with your heart," she said slowly.

"I wouldn't say that, exactly." He leaned back on the dresser. "There's a big empty place in my heart."

"How big?" She faltered.

He gave her a measuring smile. "About a size twelve would be my guess."

She nodded slowly. "Fourteen."

"Marry me, Callie."

Automatically she started to laugh then stopped herself. "Are you serious?"

He gave her a warning look.

"Bret. It's too soon. My divorce was only finalized last week."

"Too soon!" He looked like he would explode. "I've waited fourteen years, Callie. And you're telling me it's too soon? I asked you to the Valentine's Dance! That was back in high school! Because I loved you. And you turned me down.

"I loved you when we were kids, before that damned play, even. Before you kissed me—fourteen times. I've been telling you for years, Callie. And you haven't been listening.

"How long did you go out with Richard before you married him? Three years? And your marriage lasted four. You gave the wrong man seven years! I could have told you in three minutes and saved you the trouble." He threw the towel at the floor. "I can tell you, now, who the right man is. I'm not waiting three more years. I'm not waiting three more minutes. Marry me, Callie. Marry me and tell me I haven't wasted all these years, waiting."

She gave him a small, warm smile of encouragement.

His expression softened. "So what do you say…Miss February? Will you be my Valentine…for the rest of my life?"

"I don't know," she demurred, but he knew he'd won. "You're hard on clothes," she teased. "I don't mind the panties, but that pink dress was brand new."

"So how much do I owe you for the dress?" he said, his voice pleased and not the least bit apologetic.

"The rest of your life," she told him.

Miss December

ജ

Chapter One

ꟹ

"Your November assignment is having trouble adjusting, Hardin. You're sure…you followed the handbook?"

The agent lifted his smoldering gaze to burn into Davis. "You've seen the visual documents," he told her.

Davis nodded, leaving her thoughts unspoken. It wasn't difficult to doctor a visual document.

"I've always been straight with you, Davis."

"I know." Davis sighed then shrugged at the man seated before her. "I'm sorry. It's not like this hasn't happened in the past. It's not like your students haven't fallen for you before. But November's having trouble settling in with her new mate. And this month's lift goes out tomorrow."

"I'll see her," he stated curtly.

"Thank you," she said, then gave him a sly grin. "I'd appreciate it…if it isn't too much trouble."

Hardin returned her gaze almost coldly. "No trouble at all."

Davis nodded again as she considered the man seated on the other side of her desk in the sterile white office. "You've gotten serious in your old age, Hardin. I remember when…" but she left the statement unfinished. Quietly she considered the man seated across from her.

At thirty-two, Hardin had proven to be the best of her agents. Tall and leanly muscled with a thick mane of waving black hair, his European features were ruggedly chiseled in a dark face. It wasn't hard to understand why he was so successful with his students—and that was *before* he turned his brilliant blue gaze on them to burn from beneath dark, brooding eyebrows. He had an inviting mouth, she decided—long and hard and masculine, with a generous, sulky bottom lip. "Thank you," she repeated with sincerity. "Will you see her alone?"

"No." Hardin shook his head. "Have her man accompany her."

"Do you want payment for November on plastic or on your hand?"

Hardin extended his hand in answer and Davis ran her palmwand over the heel of his palm, where his invisible palmcode was permanently imprinted on his skin.

"Thank you for your work," Davis concluded. "Your next assignment will be in your cube tomorrow evening."

"December," Hardin said quietly.

"Yes," Davis answered. "We're wrapping up this segment of the project at the end of the year. This will be your last chance to get in under the wire."

"I understand."

"Good luck, Hardin."

"Thank you, sir."

Davis stood when he did. "If you're ready, you'll find November in Room Eight."

He nodded vaguely, his eyes unfocused, his mind clearly not on November as he turned and left his supervisor's office.

* * * * *

The woman was upon him before he could even close the door. Hardin looked down on the attractive, leggy blonde who was clinging to him, then lifted his eyes to connect with the man across the room. Her mate. Standing between the bed and the full-length virtual window, the redhead returned his gaze coldly, without smiling.

Pulling the woman's face out of his chest, Hardin thumbed the tears from beneath her eyes as he held her face and he kissed her. When her eyes closed, he used the opportunity to observe her mate. With a surly expression, and his arms crossed over his chest, the man turned to face the virtual window. The window's golden light accented his hard features. His nose was straight, his cheekbones high, his face lean, his jaw very square and his mouth set in a glowering straight line.

Good, Hardin thought. This was a situation he could work with.

Breaking the kiss, he put his finger on November's lush, trembling lips to silence her a moment. "Is this your chosen mate?" he asked her.

She nodded.

"What's he like?"

"He's not you," she said immediately.

He let the long line of his mouth curve into a smile. "Introduce me to him."

The girl looked uncertainly between the two men.

"Introduce us. I want to meet him."

With both hands behind her, clasping one of Hardin's, the blonde pulled him toward the tall redhead who turned from the window to give him a cynical stare.

"This is Weston," she introduced her mate. "Weston, this is...my mentor. This is the man I love."

Before the redhead had a chance to react, Hardin had reached out, grasped his hand and shaken it. Then with a yank, he pulled himself close to the man and put his mouth at Weston's ear. "Don't let me get away with anything," he whispered in a rough command.

Grinning at the man's wary expression, Hardin took a step backward and delivered his next words without looking at the woman beside him. His eyes skimmed the redhead up and down. "He looks like he ought to do, November," Hardin delivered with very deliberate male arrogance.

"I don't want to talk about him."

"But didn't you choose him?"

"Yes, but it's not working out." Tears rippled in her eyes as she clung to Hardin's side.

He gave her a quiet smile of sympathy. "Do you want to leave the project?"

"No! No," she repeated quickly. At his side, he felt her shudder. "I don't ever want to go back to…the way it was before."

"Then you're going to have to make it work," he told her gently. "You know I'm not a mate candidate."

She shook her head. "But *why*?" she asked, her voice cracking.

"I'm not fertile," he told her. "You know that, sweetheart. Have you given him a chance—"

"No," the redhead broke in abruptly.

"You haven't laid him yet?"

Grimly, Weston shook his head as his eyes narrowed accusingly on the girl.

Pulling November in front of him, Hardin took her by the lapels of her plain white blouse and smoothed his thumbs over the crisp fabric between his fingers. "Why don't I help you two get started," he suggested, cutting a hard grin at Weston as he reached for the top button of her shirt and popped it open.

Almost frantically, the woman shook her head. "I want *you*," she protested. "I want *you* to make love to me."

"I will," he told her. "But it will have to be the last time. Do you understand?" He cupped her chin in one hand as she nodded up at him. "I won't leave you with my memory alone," he continued gently. "Weston has to be involved as well. That's the condition under which I came here. To demonstrate that you can be happy with your mate."

"But…don't you *care* about me?"

"Of course I care about you," he soothed, "but I don't love you. For me, you're only one in a large number of students, all of whom I care for—but none of whom I care for passionately."

The redhead's jaw hardened while Hardin popped the second button, then Weston crossed the room to shove him aside. Grabbing a handful of blouse, Weston worked the next button loose himself while Hardin let his eyes slip down to November's breasts a lingering moment. Shooting a smile at the girl before he moved behind her, he pulled her blouse open and, as Weston got the buttons undone, he played his fingers across the girl's pale, silky skin, dragging the blouse down over her shoulders. When Weston glared into his face, Hardin dropped his eyes into the girl's cleavage, raising his eyebrows and lifting his eyes again to give the man a pointed look.

As Weston returned his attention to his task and continued to work his way through the buttons, Hardin slid his palms up November's sides to cover the full rounded mounds of her bare breasts, and lowered his mouth to press against the side of her neck. The girl's head fell back on his shoulder and her eyes closed as he lifted both breasts and rolled her tender pink nipples between the rough pads of his fingertips. With a nod to Weston, he slid his hands away, allowing them to be replaced by the redhead's, and watched as the man gathered the plush, pliable weight into his hands and lowered his head to pull one of November's blushing nipples into his mouth. Tilting his head, Hardin watched the man's open mouth work greedily at November's breast. His lean cheeks hollowed as he ate hungrily at her nipple, mauling her roughly with mouth and lips and tongue.

November gasped and her back curved, instinctively feeding her breast into Weston's mouth as he suckled and rasped at her full, flushed nipple. Opening her eyes, she gazed up into Hardin's smile as she remembered herself and pulled out of her mate's embrace, then turned away from Weston to press her chest into Hardin's. He was pleased when Weston moved in close behind the girl, his groin against her backside, his hands casing her hips possessively as his lips nudged into the hair at her temple and his harsh, humid breath stirred a few curling strands to tremble on her forehead. "I don't love you," Hardin reminded her in a quiet voice. "Consider what that means, November. The man at your front can bring you to perfect orgasm without actually getting aroused himself. I might even have to pump myself a few times before I'd be hard enough to enter you.

"The man at your back," he whispered against her ear, "is hot for you. He's hard just thinking about you, just looking at you. He wants you. You know he does," he said, softly, letting his warm breath caress her skin. "You can feel him. You can feel his cock pressing between the cheeks of your ass—hard, insistent proof of his interest. Of his need for you." With these words, he trailed his tongue around the outer shell of her ear then prodded gently into her ear's opening as a long sighing moan wisped and hung on her parted lips. Catching the delicate shell of her ear between his teeth, he gave it a final nip before lifting his head.

Shooting a look of meaning at his male collaborator, Hardin reached for the bottom of November's straight, knee-length skirt. Together, the two men rucked the stiff fabric up her legs, their hands competing to lead and dominate as their fingers wrapped the girl's long slender thighs. Hardin played his palms over her sparely covered pelvic wings while Weston's gaze dipped to watch his own hands smooth over the girl's naked cheeks, exposed and divided by the lace thong she wore.

"Do you want that?" Hardin asked gently. "Will you settle for that? Will you settle for sex without love, without passion? Will you settle for my perfect timing, the result of my *perfect* disinterest, when you could have the spontaneity, heat and excitement only *this* man can offer you? When you could have a man's rough touch, unanticipated and out of control, stunning your body into unexpected bliss?

"Do you want *me* to slip your lace thong down your legs with expert finesse, November? Or do you want a man to yank them past your sex in an urgent demand to reach you—to have you—and take you, eager to get his cock up against you, rub his damp flesh against yours and mark you with his scent as he drags his streaming cock head over your belly and rubs his cum into your skin? Do you want *me* gentling you? Or do you want a man crushing into you and taking you without refinement, without reserve, without planning and completely without control?"

Hardin was aware that Weston was working her thong down over her hips, and he let him. Sliding a palm over her flat, bared stomach, Hardin slipped two fingers through the dainty curls on her rise and into the top of her cleft. Intruding between her pink pussy lips, he dipped and swirled his thick fingers into the velvet warmth of her sex.

"You're wet," he stated softly. "But who are you wet for, November? The man at your front or the man at your back?"

"You," she sobbed in a soft moan as his fingers slid between her labia to explore the damp folds of her sex with a fine control and meticulous care.

"Are you sure?" he whispered. "What feels better, November? My fingers toying with your clit or the thick length of his cock prodding between the cheeks of your ass? Because—you should know, November—while I'm *playing* with your sex, the man behind you *isn't* playing. He's dead serious. Dead serious about getting between your legs and planting his cock deep inside your cunt, reaming into you, banging into you and claiming you in a way that will make my *sex play* seem a pale game in comparison.

"Open your legs, sweetheart. Open your legs for me. Open your legs for *him*."

With a breathless sound that was scorched with need, November tried to comply but was hampered by the lace thong stretching tight across her thighs. A harsh curse followed from Weston, then a wrench of sound indicating he'd torn her panties off to get to her. Hardin slipped his fingers through the tender line of her soft, wet seam and smiled when he brushed knuckles with Weston.

Eager and aroused, his breath raging out of his chest, the redhead was intent on prying her legs apart with his large hands. Gently, Hardin continued to finger her clit, while Weston parted his fly and brought his dick into play. Seconds later, Hardin's fingers bumped up against the thick cock head Weston was now pushing through her folds from behind her. When Weston pulled back, Hardin smiled slyly as he slid his hand deeper into her pussy and pressed two fingertips against her opening.

He was pushing it, he realized. Pushing the man at her back.

Trying for her vulva, Weston's cock head nudged up against Hardin's fingers and from the redhead's throat came a growl of warning as he tried to take her vagina from behind. There was a moment's silence as the man glared at him. "Get your fingers out of her cunt," he snarled. "The woman is mine! And her *name* is Sylvie, you arrogant bastard."

Hardin felt a shiver go through the girl and smiled, knowing that tremor of excitement was for the man fighting to claim her. Slowly, he pulled his fingers up through her wet folds to the front of her pussy, where he continued to gently massage her fattened lips with a light friction while, at the same time, Weston entered her with a harsh guttural grunt.

November met this sound with a gasp and Weston tightened his grip on her waist as he pumped his hips into the space between her legs.

Dropping to his knees, Hardin put his lips at the top of her parting cleft, planting a long, suckling kiss on the clit he exposed between the thumbs that spread her labia before gently lashing the ripe bud of flesh with the rough tip of his tongue.

"Oh my Lord," November whispered, inching her legs wider as she grasped Hardin's shoulders and leaned forward a little, arching her back to receive Weston's cock more deeply. "Oh my Lord," she repeated, her eyes wide, her teeth worrying her bottom lip as she turned her head to stare at the ginger curls at Weston's groin, to watch his thick root retract several inches then slam into her again. Her eyes lifted to her mate's face where she watched his lips twist, his eyes narrow with each thrust he brought against the rounded globes of her bottom, watched his eyes focus on the root of his own cock, then watched his gaze lift to meet hers.

Without warning, she was yanked away from Hardin's face as Weston lifted her off his dick and turned her to face him, crowding her toward the room's bed. November backed up before the man's advance as he edged her closer to the bed. One of his hands clutched the top of his pants, while the other wrapped around the long, flushed length of his cock. Seconds later, November was laid out on the bed and Weston was thrusting between her legs as she whispered and murmured and pleaded, goading her mate forward.

With a hand on the door lever, Hardin grinned as he watched November's legs wrap around Weston's hips, her hands pulling at his buttocks, urging his hips to plow and take and fornicate her open pussy. Her low choking moans were a clear indication of her need—and of her choice.

Davis was waiting on the other side of the door as Hardin pulled it closed behind him. He shot her a hard grin. "Another satisfied customer," he imparted. "You catch any of that?"

"All of it." Davis nodded. "You certainly have a way with words, Hardin. I hope it helps you with your next assignment."

Hardin nodded, rubbing the back of his neck. "Thanks," he threw over his shoulder as his long legs took him down the hall.

Chapter Two

ꕥ

Wearily, Hardin opened the door to his cube. When he closed it behind him, he leaned against the door, staring into the room without seeing. December. It had been a long year, he thought, then pushed himself away from the door to walk across the room toward his small kitchen. Stopping at his system panel on the counter, he pushed a few buttons, grabbed an unmarked bottle and poured himself a short drink of unauthorized alcohol. On the other side of the cast-iron counter, the visual document he'd called up opened on his aluminum coffee table and for a moment he stared at it before reaching into the cupboard for a can. Absently, his attention fixed on the visual, he reached for his drink and swallowed the liquor then went through the movements of opening the can and finding a spoon. Carrying his dinner out of his kitchen-eat, he set his food on the low table where a small image of a woman leaned back on her elbows and spread her legs on the table's smooth surface. Tilting his head, he frowned at her. She wore nothing but a pair of electric blue panties that were a brilliant splash of color across the pale curve of her full hips.

Returning to his kitchen, he poured himself another drink and carried it back to place it on the low table beside the woman's image. Dropping onto his dark leather couch and picking up the can again, he watched the document. He was halfway through his meal before he ordered, "Replay 90." Immediately, the visual document backed up ninety seconds and replayed as he watched.

The room was silent except for the thick rasp of his breath and the occasional command to back the visual and replay. Without finishing his meal, he placed the can on the table as, stretching back on the couch, he dug his fingers into his crotch and rearranged the thick pile of sex at his groin. Several minutes later he stood and, without removing his eyes from the visual, he headed across the room to his dressing case, shuffling through the top drawer.

Frowning suddenly, he pulled his eyes from the document and slammed the drawer shut, then yanked at the drawer below it. A frenzied search produced nothing and he dropped to his knees as he moved on down to the next drawer.

A breath of relief filled his lungs as he reached into the drawer, then headed back to the couch with a pair of silk panties clutched in his large fist. Throwing himself at the couch, he sprawled on his back, and lifted a knee to rest against the back of the couch as he continued to watch the visual at the same time that he used his left hand to pull his fly open. There was a faint ripping sound as the adhesive strips parted, then he reached into his slacks to pull out the long, heavy weight of his cock. Rubbing the silk panties against the edge of his mouth, he put one foot on the floor and let his legs fall open as his right hand traveled slowly down his body and over his groin where he wrapped the scrap of pale blue silk around his straining erection. Pumping himself slowly with his right hand, his left curled to hold and finger his balls.

For a long time he watched the image on the table, his right hand wrapped around his dick and moving with increasing velocity as he forced his cock toward completion, his breath growing more ragged with each frictioning drag of his fist.

Abruptly, he stopped—blinking hard.

With his breath harsh and laboring in his chest, he got to his feet and took two stiff steps toward the projected image. Choking down on his flesh, his fingers gripped his dick then started moving again. Pistoning his hand down the length of his cock, Hardin's eyes were glued to the tiny woman sprawled on the table as his dick flashed and spurted to splash at the image. As he continued the punishing action of his fist, he levered his shaft downward and his cock continued to surge and empty onto the table. Eyes blinking, chin on his heaving chest, he considered the product of his lust shining on the long aluminum coffee table—a large erotic puddle glinting between the splayed legs of the tiny woman displayed in the visual document.

Rousing himself with a shake, he used the panties to wipe the table then headed for the facility where he splurged on a three-minute shower, using at least one full minute of that time to thoroughly wash the pale blue scrap of silk. The panties were in his hand as he exited the facility. Three seconds in his micro dried the underwear and he rubbed them against his cheek as he crossed the room, then returned them to the top drawer of his dressing case.

Pushing the drawer closed, he blew out a sigh as he turned and considered his room. The rest of the evening he spent straightening and cleaning his cube in preparation for his new student, who would be arriving in approximately twenty hours.

* * * * *

Twenty hours later, Hardin was turning out of the elevair and striding down the corridor toward his cube. Stopping outside his door, he reached for the handle and held it a second while the electronic eye read his palmcode. When the handle glowed green, he pushed the lever down.

Hardin drew in a breath and held it, blinking as he closed the door behind him. Quietly, he stood watching the woman tied to his bed—his assignment for December. Although she appeared drowsy, she was awake—the drug used during her abduction was just beginning to wear off.

As he'd requested, she'd been stripped down to her panties. He tilted his head as he observed her. They were plain white cotton bikinis.

As he watched her, she shook her head several times, trying to focus on him while she squirmed to maneuver herself into a sitting position. At that point, she realized she was bound to the bed's headboard. Her mouth dropped open in quiet surprise as she frowned at her bindings then returned her puzzled gaze to his face.

Hardin continued to stare as his blood pounded dully in the background, surged through his veins and rested heavily in his groin.

She was unlike other women. In a world populated with physically perfect humans, this woman stood apart. In this day and age—his day and age—women were uniformly beautiful, turned out of the Uterine Labs like plastic baby dolls to grow into perfect mannequins with long slender legs supporting designer-name bodies. Their facial features were artistically composed to please the eye. Their eye color, skin color and lips were all carefully coordinated—chic accessories for their perfectly molded faces.

But this woman was none of those things. Her body was lush, generous and soft. Her alley cat eyes were filled with a keen intelligence absent in most beautifully empty faces. Her lips were a dark smear of red on a face several shades too white. Her hair was neither gold nor ebony nor fire. Instead it was autumn leaves chasing the sun.

In short, she was an anomaly, a bit of a lab error, a less-than-perfect human being who had somehow squeezed through the cracks during the birth process.

Finally expelling the breath he held, Hardin tilted his head to the other side and watched her with intense interest. He knew she would surprise him with almost every word, every action. She would have a cutting wit and, even more exciting, a bit of a temper. Initially, she would fight him but when she finally gave in, there'd be a level of sinful eroticism in her surrender that would scorch his balls and reduce his dick to a lovesick lapdog. He knew that when he finally got his mouth between her legs, she'd taste like sweet sin, dark and intoxicatingly addictive. And when he finally took her, he'd drown himself in the deep, soft folds of her body as she surrounded his sex in her thick, hot, liquid heat, racking his cock away from his body, her thick pussy wedged between his dick and his groin as the cushioned length of her vagina enveloped him in a luscious fleshy hug and his balls pressed against the warm, full pillows of her ass.

And when she came! When she came, the plush line of her cunt would close on him and brutalize his shaft in a tight, unforgiving fist. Inside the hot clasp of her sheath, long, pulling pulses would suck his cock to completion, forcing him through a blisteringly hot orgasm nothing less than soul-scalding. He'd shoot into her as he threw his hips at her, taking her as deeply as he could, as hard as he could, slamming into her and holding hard inside her clenching channel as his head hung over hers and his cock emptied inside her.

And afterward, after he'd filled her with his cum and her cunt had taken everything he could throw at her—and everything she could bear—he'd fall asleep beside her, his cock head resting just inside her vulva, his lips on her forehead, one hand spread out to clutch her bottom while his other caged one of her rouge-tipped breasts, his body pressed against hers, demanding, even in sleep, to claim every inch of contact humanly possible.

She was what an agent like he would consider a natural. She was born to copulate. Without thinking, he licked his lips and rubbed them together in a restless gesture of unslaked hunger, thirsting to latch onto the puffy mounds of her nipples and draw one of them halfway down his throat with a rough sucking statement of possession. Everything inside him shifted, became edgy and needy as his hand clamped on the door handle behind him and he fought his body's demand to get his hands on her soft, giving flesh, to pull her under his body, get on her and get his dick inside her.

With his eyes resting on the rounded flesh of her hip, he pictured himself between her legs, pulling her thighs wide, watching the lips of her sex as they parted, moist and creaming as he slid his hands up the inside of her legs. He imagined his hands teasing lightly at the outer fringes of her sex, playing through the dark cloud of curls on her mound and dropping into her pussy as he opened her with his fingers and dragged them up through her thick, swollen folds until her body twisted with need.

His eyes closed as he held the image in his mind—his hand spread in the small of her back as he rose over her, spread her wider with his knees, and took her cunt with a deep thrust of his thick, rigid cock, fighting his way to the back of her vagina, stretching into her luxurious velvet-lined channel with a brutal thrust of his hips. Ripping into her as her cunt rippled around his erection and milked—hard. Milked him to a head as his cock erupted and flashed inside her, pumping her channel full of his release.

Filled with the fiendish urge to penetrate and pump, Hardin's fist tightened on the door handle as his cock thickened and he fought the inclination to straighten his penis with his hand. He didn't want to alarm her.

*****

Pulling her bottom lip through her teeth, Kansas narrowed her gaze on the man across the room, standing just inside the door. He was beautiful, but then most men were. Generations of genetic refining had produced humans with pleasing proportions, coordinated eye-skin color and a *lot* of blondes. This man was dark, however. Black hair and blue eyes. Internally, Kansas shrugged. There were plenty of those, as well.

He wasn't so much different than any other regular, everyday male beauty. Except perhaps for the deep, haunting glow in his eyes, alive and vital and just about on fire as his gaze burned down her body like a lick of flame. A few strands of his waving hair slid down his forehead to screen eyes that blazed like storm-swept, tropical seas.

He was attired in the best that standard issue could offer. His T-shirt was very white and new and looked expensively soft where it clung to the muscles that ripped across his chest. His black canvas slacks hugged his long legs loosely but lovingly as they stretched down his calves to bunch in a few folds above his dark slip-ons.

As he stood there, his hard, curving lips tipped upward at one corner then parted to give her a reassuring smile that exposed the edge of his very straight, very white teeth. Automatically, Kansas pressed her lips together in an unconscious attempt to hide her own somewhat-less-than-perfect teeth. Two hundred years ago, they'd have never even been noticed. Today, the slightest flaw was considered an eyesore.

Despite the fact that she had woken to find herself almost naked and tied to a large bed, she wasn't exactly afraid. Violence, aggression, and even passion had long since been bred out of humans. There was no such thing as murder anymore, although she'd read of it in some very ancient 'tronic books still available at black-market sites. She'd read about anger and fighting—war—and agreed they were barbaric. The suffering they'd caused was the reason certain human traits had been eradicated.

But she was...uneasy. Something about the man who stood smiling at her made her uncomfortable.

Or maybe it was something about *her.* In an odd way she felt unsettled within her own skin. A stranger to herself. As if a new female persona were stirring to life within her, blinking its eyes open to an intense, unsettling emotional awareness of the very masculine creature standing before her.

"How do you feel?" he asked, and she was surprised by her body's warm response to the sound of that deep, rich rumble.

"I'm just a little cold."

"I'm sorry. I'd forgotten that you—just let me adjust the climate."

His long legs took him across the room to his counter where he pushed a few buttons on the panel set into the cast-iron surface.

Licking her bottom lip, Kansas took in the room.

At twenty-five feet by perhaps twenty, his cube was *huge* by any standards—at least four times the size of the cube she shared with three other people. He actually had what looked to be his own kitchen-eat as opposed to the food delivery chute in place at her own cubeblock. What was even more amazing was the window. Although the lower portion of the window was covered by a full blind, blocking any view it might provide, a glorious wedge of light shot through the top portion of the large rectangle where a wide strip of clear glass confirmed it was a real window, not a virtual window like the small oval in her cube. Following government edicts meant to ensure the conservation of natural resources—and considered an unnecessary waste of energy—glass windows had been pretty much designed out of buildings long before her production date. Virtual windows could be programmed to present a precisely accurate view of the outside, but most people selected an enhanced view—everything in the same place, but cleaner, brighter, prettier and more colorful.

The man would have to be a government contractor, Kansas decided, making at least two mil a month. "If I had my clothing back, I might be warmer," she suggested, hoping it didn't sound like she was arguing.

"I can't do that," he told her.

"Why?"

His head came up quickly and he turned to look at her, a warm, interested fire in his eyes, as though she'd said something delightfully amusing. "I'll explain everything in time."

"Can you explain," again she hesitated, "why I'm tied?"

He nodded and smiled, a wicked affair that made her shiver—a strange and unexpected sensation.

"To keep you from leaving."

She nodded. This seemed like a reasonable explanation, if somewhat…insufficient. She fought the urge to argue, knowing that no one else argued, knowing that she wasn't *supposed* to argue. It was this tendency of hers to question, along with her appearance, which labeled her an anomaly amongst her coworkers. Something had probably fallen through the cracks when her DNA was arranged.

A lot, actually.

A lot had fallen through the cracks. She was too large. Too tall as well as too wide. It was almost impossible to find clothes to fit her in the standard issue outlets. Her hair was neither blonde nor sable nor auburn nor chestnut. Instead, it was somewhere between the color of straw and dry windblown leaves. And her eyes, which probably should have been blue or green, if everything had gone according to plan, were brown rims on greenish centers.

The three men she shared her cell with were, like her, just a wee bit on the anomaly side of normal. Just...*not quite* like everyone else. And everyone else was pretty much uniformly the same. Beautiful, trim, evenly proportioned with rich hair tones and vibrant eye colors—just like the man standing before her.

"I'm hungry," she told him and he nodded apologetically.

"I'm sorry," he said, "but you can't eat today—or tomorrow."

Kansas thought about this for several moments before daring the question. She'd never gone a day without eating before. "Why?"

The man strode toward her and pulled a chair up close to the bed's edge as he dropped into it. "Because of the inhibitors." This time he didn't wait for her question before going on. "All of the food in our food delivery systems is charged with inhibitors."

"Inhibitors?"

"To inhibit off-standard behavior," he told her.

Frowning at him, she tried to understand. "What do you mean by off-standard behavior?"

He sprawled in the wide, comfortable chair with his legs open, a natural stance for males and her eyes settled on one of his knees. She'd always thought it strange that, even after ten generations of human life without sex, a woman would still cross her legs when she sat and a man would open his—wide. The woman always circumspect and withholding. The man always available and offering. Her eyes were drawn to a flash of light and her gaze slid sideways to rest between his legs, where a bright brass rivet shone at the very base of his fly. Purely functional and meant to hold the thick layers of canvas together, it nonetheless seemed artfully placed. For some reason, she couldn't pull her eyes from the interesting point of light. His eyes followed hers into his crotch and she watched his fingers stroke the rivet a few times before sliding up over the thick mound at his groin.

"The inhibitors stifle any natural…passion you may have."

"Passion?" she exclaimed immediately. "But that doesn't happen anymore. Passion, violence, anger and jealousy are stripped from our DNA during our birth design."

"I'm not talking about that kind of passion," he told her quietly and went on to explain. "I'm talking about the body's natural physical response to…arousing stimuli." He took a deep breath. "I'm talking about sex."

Kansas felt her eyes grow wide. "Sex!" she exclaimed, finally nervous. "Sex is obscene! Nobody does sex anymore. Nobody *normal*! There's no need. People are designed and generated in Uterine Labs! Why would anyone *want* to have sex? It's dangerous, dirty and…and messy. It's porno…it's porno…technic!"

"Pornographic," he corrected her gently as he nodded and a few strands of black hair slipped down to shadow his left eye. "That's what a lifetime of education has led us to believe. You're right. Most people—normal people—don't do sex, although you must know it's available on the black market for a price. And you might have heard about fasters—people who starve themselves for several days and do dark things to themselves…as well as others.

"But you've been brought to me to be reconditioned. I'm going to change your mind about sex. Are you afraid?"

"Yes, I'm afraid," she shot back and realized immediately that was a mistake. A normal woman wouldn't have been afraid. Puzzled perhaps, confused, but not afraid.

Kansas had spent the entirety of her existence trying to fit in, trying to be normal and she was damned if she was going to let this man destroy a lifetime of work. Dabbling in, *even talking about sex,* would move her right out of the Anomaly Category on the social scale and straight into the Shunned for Life Category. "Are you going to do sex to me?" she squeaked with a hard swallow; her chin trembling as she pulled on the wide straps that bound her wrists to the bed's headboard.

The man grimaced. "We're going to do it together."

Now she was alarmed! Now she struggled. Scrambling back on the bed until her bottom was competing for a place amongst the pillows, she pulled on the bindings that spread her arms and fixed her wrists to the headboard. Frantically, her eyes went around the room, looking for some means of escape. "Listen," she said anxiously. "You look like a nice man, a normal man—"

"I'm not," he cut her off. "I'm not normal. At least not what you've come to believe is normal. You live with three men," he said abruptly.

"Y-yes?"

"And they're normal?"

"Next to you? Yes! They're *infinitely* normal."

He blew out an impatient breath. "Have you ever noticed them?"

"Have I ever— *What*?"

"Have you ever noticed them? Have you ever been aware of them? Have you ever been interested in them? Have you ever looked at one of them and felt…anything?"

"Anything like what?"

"*Anything at all!* You've seen them naked." He challenged her, almost angrily. "When they were naked did you ever feel anything…here?"

Kansas followed his hand as it dropped into his groin and cupped to hold the heavy mass of male equipment inside his dark canvas slacks.

"No," she answered immediately, though she felt her cheeks warm.

It was almost the truth, she told herself. Only…her version of the truth was just a shade imperfect—like everything else about her. One of her cubemates—Jansen. Some mornings he would wake up hard. His penis. It would soften again after he used the facility, but while it was hard, she would find her eyes drawn to the long, stiff flesh swinging at the bottom of his lean torso. And she felt…something. Something hard to describe. Something that tickled her senses deep within. Something like hunger or thirst.

She would order a soft drink along with something to eat.

It always went away…eventually.

"No," she repeated stubbornly and the man's mouth curled up at one side in a challenging smile. He didn't believe her.

"You'll be with me a week," he informed her. "And during that time I'll be your instructor."

"My instructor?"

He smiled at the interruption as though she couldn't have said anything that could have pleased him more.

"Yes," he said. "I'm going to awaken you. I'm going to teach you how to feel."

Chapter Three

ℰ𝒪

"You'll call me mentor," he instructed her brusquely. "And I'll refer to you as December." Evidently anticipating her next question, he held up his hand. "You'll never know my name and I prefer not to know yours. You're my December assignment, hence, your name.

"Let me explain what I'm going to do to you. When I'm done, I'll tell you why." He smiled at her reassuringly. "Are you warm enough?"

Edging a bit further up on the bed, increasing the distance that separated them, she nodded warily.

"For two days you won't be able to eat—today and tomorrow. That's to clear your system of the inhibitors. I won't touch you today. There'd be no sense in it since you wouldn't feel anything. Sometime tomorrow you'll reach the stage where you might be receptive to my touch."

He drew in a breath.

"Tomorrow I'll touch you," he said, his eyes glowing a soft blue fire, and she wondered at the awed tone of reverence in his voice just before he shook his head and his eyes focused on hers again. "Nothing alarming," he added quickly. "Just my fingers on your lips, across the side of your breast perhaps, or along your hips. If you respond well to that, I might smooth my hand down over your bottom and…pull you against me."

Her chest rose and fell with thick, heavy breaths, which she attributed to fear. "Why?" she croaked out in a soft whisper. "Why would you do that?"

"Because it will feel good," he explained to her gently. "The next day, we'll try a kiss."

"A kiss?"

He nodded patiently. "I'll touch your lips with mine." His eyes slid down her neck to rest on her breasts. "I'll...touch you other places as well—with my lips."

She shook her head at him, certain he was mad.

"I'll run my lips into the hollow at the base of your neck and kiss the pulse that rests just beneath your smooth, satin skin. I'll kiss your nipples, your breasts. I'll spend a long time on your nipples," he murmured as his legs shifted further apart. "Then I'll go to work on your belly button. I might even use my tongue."

"And you think I'm going to *sit still* for all this?"

He shrugged. "Probably not. You'll remain bound and tied until I'm certain you won't run."

"Until you're certain I won't run? That will never happen," she stated with fire.

His nostrils flared and his eyes flamed an instant before he dragged his gaze from her chest and refocused on her eyes. "It will happen sooner than you think," he soothed. "On the third day, you'll see me naked. I'll lie beside you and let you get used to me undressed. I'll...touch you just about everywhere. And I'll kiss you everywhere I've kissed you before, as well as a few new places. We won't take the next step until I'm sure you're ready."

"Ready?" Kansas asked, dismayed at the tremor of alarm easily discerned in her voice.

"On the fourth day, I'll open your legs," he said in a soft rush of breath. "And we'll see how far we get. If I can get you wet with a little rubbing and touching—"

"Wet?"

"Your opening, your vagina, will dampen when you're aroused. It will be your body's way of preparing itself for a man's entry. If I can get you wet," he continued, "I'll let you feel my cock nudging through your folds. This is all new to you, and strange, but I can assure you it will feel good in a way you've never experienced before. We'll go slowly and I won't give you any more than you can take.

"On the fifth day, I'll taste you. I'll finger you first. I'll prepare you with my fingers," he explained when she frowned at him. "I'll use my fingers between your legs. I'll finger your labia open and play with your pink, folded sex until you writhe beneath my hand and my fingers are sliding through your wet pussy. Then I'll go down on you. I'll put my head between your legs and take your sex in my mouth." He gave her a warm smile. "I'll use my tongue and lips to kiss and suck and lick into your pussy. I'll do that until I feel the inside of your legs relax, until you open for me."

"Open for you?" she choked out.

He nodded. "At some point, you'll stop fighting. I'll know when that happens. Your body will tighten with excitement and need but your legs will relax and open in a natural plea for a man rising to take you. Your pussy will be sweet and wet, your cunt soft, aching for a cock stretching inside it.

"Then we'll stop," he delivered abruptly.

Despite herself, a wisp of a groan escaped her lips.

In response, he tilted his head to observe her, his expression suspicious. "Before the end of the week," he finally continued, "you'll have your first orgasm."

Breathlessly, she shook her head. "Orgasm. What's that?"

The man's eyes closed as his fingertips came together and his lips thinned between his teeth. "What's the best thing that's ever happened to you?" he queried from behind closed eyes. When she didn't answer, he made some suggestions "Chocolate? Laughter? Sunshine? Imagine sharing all of those things with your favorite person—only raised to a magnitude of ten." He opened his eyes and smiled. "That's the feeling just before orgasm. Raise that another several magnitudes and you're climaxing, sobbing with pleasure at the point of release."

He nodded his head wryly at her expression of disbelief. "Your vagina will be open and streaming, clutching on empty air, gasping for something, some sort of fulfillment you can't put into words. As you approach orgasm, you'll want something inside you. A man. A man's thick, hard flesh. His cock taken hard and deep inside your cunt."

"Sex," she breathed in a whisper.

"Yes," he answered with an encouraging smile. "Sex. But it won't happen that way the first time. The first time you orgasm, you'll have to go there alone, without me."

"What do you mean?"

"I can't be responsible for your first orgasm. I can take you close. Very close. But you'll have to take yourself the last few delicious touches over the edge toward climax."

She was silent for several moments. "You can't be responsible," she stated with more than a little of the fire that was always getting her into trouble. "You've abducted me against my will, taken me from my cube and my work, deprived me of my clothing, tied me to your bed and you can't be responsible? For what? What's left…*mentor*?" She forced the title out with more than a little cynicism. "You don't want to get your hands dirty? You don't want to be responsible for…attack…rape?" She grappled with the ancient words, not entirely certain of their meaning.

His eyebrows arched slightly as her conclusions appeared to surprise him. He shook his head. "It's not that, December. It won't be anything like rape, sweetheart. You'll beg me to enter you before I'll give you my cock. I won't push my cock between your legs before you ask for it." He shook his head again. "That's not the problem, at all, December."

He took a long breath.

"I can't be responsible…for you falling in love with me."

"Falling in *love* with you?"

He nodded, his expression bordering on guilty. "Do you know what I mean by love?" he asked keenly.

"Of course," she snapped just before she relented with a toss of her head. "At least I think I know," she muttered. "Some people who work with children grow to love them," she said, but even to her own ears it sounded more like a guess. "Some people—people with money—have pets."

"That's right," he encouraged her. "It's like that except…much stronger."

"Better?"

His eyebrows came together and she thought she caught a glimpse of pain in the shadowed depth of his blue gaze.

"Stronger," he repeated. "Like…you'd do anything to keep it—anything—including die for it. Lie for it. Steal for it. Even kill for it, if you were given no other choice."

"Passion," she breathed with slow revelation. "Love and…sex…result in passion! That's it, isn't it? That's why we don't do it anymore. It's dangerous!"

"That's it," he agreed with an almost weary nod. "And I won't tell you it isn't dangerous."

"Then, why?" her voice pleaded for understanding. "Why are you going to *do* this to me?"

"We have no choice…anymore."

"*We*?" Wildly, Kansas scanned the room, knowing at the same time she wouldn't be able to identify a sophisticated hidden surveillance system. "We?"

"I work for a government contractor," he said, standing. "Let me start the document." Moving to the counter he pushed a few buttons then turned to watch the visual coming up on the long aluminum coffee table.

For several moments, Kansas watched silently while a nightmare unfolded in the air before her eyes. When she shook her head in horror, he punched a button and the visual faded. "That was a Uterine Lab," he said grimly.

"What...what was wrong with them—the babies?"

"It's been going on for several years," he told her. "You may have noticed that there have been no very young children on the streets, in the parks."

She nodded.

"There are no new children coming out of the labs. As the visual demonstrated, the children are...defective. Most of them don't live more than a few hours."

Kansas watched the man as his throat worked for the next few words. "It's hard to watch," he admitted in a low voice. "I'm sorry you had to see it. But it's the only way to explain why this is happening to you, why the government is paying a high profile contractor to hire agents like me—to deliver men and women whom the contractors have established are fertile."

The man's shoulders dropped as he shook his head reluctantly.

"Willing women," he corrected his earlier statement. "Women who have been 'awakened'. Women who have relearned how to feel, who have rediscovered sex, who like sex and want to have sex. Women who don't feel guilty or dirty about it, despite a lifetime of conditioning. Women who have been convinced by men like me that sex *isn't* obscene, *isn't* pornographic. Women who can bear and rear the next generation of children.

"And while you're here, being awakened, female agents are working on male counterparts—men who are being prepared as potential mates for…you."

"But—"

"The genetics started going wrong generations ago. It's too late to unwind the DNA. The scientists have been forced to return to the beginning. It's something they should never have meddled with in the first place and can't be undone."

"But…why not just stop the inhibitors? Why not let everyone…revert?"

"The effect of inhibitors on both men and women—in their food, in their soft drinks—have made most humans sterile or almost sterile. Believe me, December, there's no other way. If there were—"

"What? You wouldn't be doing this?"

His eyes lit briefly as he grinned slowly. "I didn't say that."

* * * * *

"Are you thirsty?" he asked suddenly. When she nodded, he headed for his tiny kitchen-eat. "I'll get you a drink, then untie you so you can use the facility." Pouring water from a bottle, he rattled on. "The food you eat here is clear of inhibitors, though we still need to purge your system before you can eat. The water is safe anywhere," he instructed her. With a plastic cup in his hand, he headed toward her. "When you use the facility, you can close the door if you like. You can neither escape nor hurt yourself in there. There's no mirror, glass, cutters—nothing sharp," he told her warningly.

"And nothing I could use as a weapon," she summarized for him as he nodded.

"Nothing you could use to harm yourself either."

"Why would I want to do that?"

"Some women in your position have thought they'd rather die…at this point in their instruction."

"At this point. And later on?"

He smiled into the cup. "Those are the idealistic ones. The ones who fall in love." With one knee on the bed, he lowered himself carefully to sit beside her without touching her. Slowly, he maneuvered the cup to her mouth.

She found it awkward, trying to slurp a drink out of the cup he was holding, and before she was done she felt a cold splash and trickle that started at the top of her neck and snaked down to make a shining pearl of water between her breasts.

Apparently without thinking, her instructor reached out with a finger to catch the large drop of liquid rolling into her cleavage.

Her eyes cut quickly to his face as he realized his mistake. A brief flash of panic was at the back of his eyes and she could have sworn he was holding his breath. As his finger moved on her breast, she was surprised at the small tingle generated by his warm-rough touch. She watched his finger gently sweep the drop off her skin. Watched his eyes close as he sucked at that finger and gazed at her breasts with an expression of incredible longing. Then with slow, deliberate care, he lowered his mouth inexorably to her chest, using his tongue to lick up the remaining moisture gleaming between her breasts.

Again, she felt the faint tingle along with a lovely shivery warmth stirring deep inside her belly. When he lifted his eyes to hers, she stared at him, stunned. "Lord of the Republic! What was that?" she scraped out of a tight throat.

"You're so sensitive," he stated in a rasping whisper. "So responsive. You shouldn't have felt *anything*...with the inhibitors still so thick in your bloodstream."

For a moment, she thought he would reach out and touch her again, but instead he stood quickly, and placed the cup on the coffee table before he reached for the straps tied off at the headboard. "I'm sorry," he told her in suddenly clipped tones, "I shouldn't have touched you." Backing away from her, he gave her a wide path to enter the facility.

Shrugging her shoulders sardonically, she indicated the short lengths of strap hanging from her wrists as she pushed herself to the bed's edge and to her feet. "You're not concerned about me hanging myself in there?"

Distractedly, he shook his head. "There's nothing in there to hang yourself from," he told her, as though she'd been serious.

When she came out of the facility, he was waiting at the near side of the bed. Stopping just outside the door, she moved her hands behind her back. "What if I promised I wouldn't run?" she offered hopefully.

"I wouldn't believe you," he countered. "Come here."

"No."

Although this word set his eyes to smoldering, he smiled tolerantly. "Please, December. You must cooperate. I don't want to touch you until—"

"Tomorrow, I know." She lowered her eyes to the floor and then raised them in challenge. "What are you going to do if I refuse?" she asked quietly.

His jaw hardened and without hesitating, he took a step toward her, grasped the straps and pulled her toward the bed. Failing to get completely out of her way, his body brushed up against hers. Together they stopped and stared at each other in breathless surprise. His eyebrows crushed together in a frown of alarm as his gaze dropped to her chest. When her gaze followed his, she stared at her tawny nipples, stiffening proudly before her very eyes. "What on earth?" she whispered in quiet awe. Her eyes cut back to his when she heard him groan.

"No," he breathed. "*No.* This isn't supposed to be happening." As though caught in the pull of some undeniable gravitational force, he dropped the straps as his hands moved slowly upward and his flattened palms hovered in the air just a hair away from touching her nipples.

Following an instinct she didn't understand, Kansas leaned forward to press her nipples into his large, cool, outspread palms and nudged a knee up against his legs. "Tell me what you're going to do to me on day six," she murmured.

Chapter Four

ဢ

Her mentor took a step back, away from her. "On day six, I'll fuck you," he delivered harshly.

Kansas watched the man, his throat working as he appeared to battle some inner conflict. Finally, he took a step toward her, then another. His body came up against hers, herding her backward until her back was against the wall. One of his hands was on her breast, and she felt a tremor rip through his long frame as his fingers spread, clutching her generous weight into his palm as his other hand caught her behind the neck and tipped her face upward. As her large breast kept spilling out of his hand, he continually re-collected it, using the heel of his hand to coax it back into his fingers with a gentle caressing touch. A touch at odds with the rampant fire burning in the deep blue of his darkening irises.

For several instants his eyes searched hers, imploring, pleading for something she didn't immediately understand.

His touch, the breath-stealing nearness of his body, the demanding, possessive hold of his hand on her breast, awakened a slow, sluggish response in her body that warmed the triangle below her belly button. With sudden intuition she understood. He wanted her to stop him. He wanted her to stop him so he could move his plan forward in comfortable stages without this very awkward and unplanned deviation. But by the time Kansas opened her mouth to suggest a halt, he'd covered her lips with his.

The sensation was surprisingly pleasant, though the man seemed to be getting much more out of it than she. His heart hammered against her chest as his lips twisted on hers in stark hunger and his breath came in short, hard gasps. Finally he pulled away with a harsh moan of anguish. "No," he murmured in a low voice, his lips in her hair. "Not again. Not after all the women and all this time." Pressing her into the cool wall at her back, the man tried to catch his breath.

"It's vital that you achieve your first orgasm without me," he picked up his earlier thread with a croak, though his words seemed to be for himself as much as for her. "*Vital.* Do you understand that, December? Everything—*everything*—hangs on that one act."

Shaking her head, she lifted her gaze to his. "I don't understand."

"I'll explain...later. Close your eyes and I'll tell you about day six."

A thumb rasped over her nipple and the man's breath was damp, humid and warm on her temple as he continued. "After I'm certain you've orgasmed without me, we'll...do sex. I'll enter you—penetrate you—my cock in your vagina.

"December." He breathed the word like a treasured memory. "I'll teach you how to welcome sex, love sex, crave a man's cock in your pussy as we work our way through every possible position and I teach you to enjoy being fucked."

"Fucked?" she murmured. "You used that word before."

"Another word for sex," he explained in a strained whisper. "When a man enters a woman.

"We'll start simple—in this bed—while I rise over you and slide between your legs. But before the end of the day, you'll be straddling me and doing most of the work. We'll do it in that chair," he added in a rich musical rasp filled with a strange tremor. "I'll put you on my cock while I drive my hips up to fill your vagina." She heard him swallow as he pulled in his bottom lip with his tongue then dragged it through his teeth. "I'll take you on your hands and knees, here on the floor, kneeling behind you, my legs inside yours, spreading your legs, opening your cheeks, pulling your vulva wide for my penetration. I'll mount you from behind as I hold your hips. Then I'll stand you up and bend you over the counter and do the same thing."

For some reason she shivered. A small flame burned just below her belly button where she felt her pulse thicken, hard and heavy as it slugged through her veins. For a long time there was nothing but the sound of his breath, strangely harsh and loud in her ear.

"On the final day, after you've learned to enjoy sex, I'll teach you the finer details of how to arouse your mate, so that you're certain to have a steady source of pleasure. You'll learn where a man yearns to be touched, how and when. You'll be taught to please a man with your mouth and tongue and fist—all at the same time. You'll learn to suck cock and enjoy the salty tang of cum as it slides down your throat. You'll learn to hunger for the sensation of a man's release spilling over your tongue, and you'll come to covet the strength and power of a man thickening between your lips, forcing himself to the back of your throat, strong and hard and brutally thick while at the same time helplessly vulnerable between the harsh scrape of your teeth.

"And while you're here with me, learning all this, a mate is being trained to pleasure you in the same manner." On this signal, the man pulled away from her, a sigh in his throat and reluctance in his expression.

Taking her ties in his hand, he led her to the bed. Submissively, she let him retie her to the headboard. When he was done, he dropped into the chair beside the bed. As before, his legs spread open and she couldn't stop her eyes incursion into the space between his legs where the placket on his slacks lifted in a long, hard line and the glint of the brass rivet riding low on his crotch snagged her eyes and commanded her attention.

"After you leave here, you'll spend the next three weeks meeting potential mates. Men who've been awakened, aroused—as you have been. At the end of those three weeks you'll have chosen a mate. Together, you'll be relocated to a base in the Seychelles—a new, luxurious community where you'll live with your chosen mate and raise a family."

For several moments she watched him. "So that's the plan," she said with a touch of sardonic humor. "From beginning to endpoint."

He nodded, returning her smile a little apologetically. "That's the plan, as outlined in the handbook."

"Handbook?"

He nodded. "The handbook. It's rewritten and updated frequently but one thing never changes. Studies have proven that students who share their first orgasm with their instructors have a high risk of falling in love with their mentors. When that's the case, the initiates will often bail out of the project, choosing to return to their previous lives, lives within the cubeblocks, choosing to live without love and without sex, rather than select a mate and live in comfort on a spacious island—all free of charge, compliments of the world government."

"Do they *always* leave the project—the ones who fall in love with their…instructors?"

He shook his head. "Not always. But initiates who choose a mate, despite their love for their mentors, take years to settle in and achieve true happiness.

"That's why you must take yourself to your first orgasm. I don't want that to happen to—I don't want that to happen."

"You don't get paid when that's the case," she stated bluntly.

He blinked at her as though she'd slapped him, then shook his head slowly. "It's not the money," he said with a depth of emotion that was convincing even to her.

Kansas gazed at him, assessing his obviously heartfelt reaction. "Have you ever lost a student before?"

"Yes." He said it quickly with unflinching honesty, as though it were a great failing that he was too proud to hide. As though it were a personal fault that troubled him deeply, as if it were a crime that must be faced and confessed in the hopes of gaining some sort of strange absolution.

"Does an instructor ever fall in love with a student?" she asked with shrewd interest.

"No," he said in a low voice.

"No?"

"Not if he's a professional."

"Why not? Wouldn't you, for instance, want to live on a spacious island in the Seychelles, courtesy of the government?"

He lifted his haunted gaze to search hers. "I'm not a mate candidate," he told her and then went on in a rush. "I'm not a fertile male."

"You're not capable of fathering a child," she translated and he nodded in answer. "But you're capable of doing sex?"

At this he smiled.

"Are you capable of love?"

"Everyone's capable of love," he told her. "Love hasn't been bred out of humans."

Kansas struggled to comprehend. "You say that love is a strong passion—strong enough to incite murder. Yet, if you were to fall in love with one of your students, you'd...give her up? To another man?"

"Yes," he said without hesitation. "I couldn't condemn someone I loved to the alternative—the alternative of living a cubelife without feeling, without love, without anything." His gaze moved to the floor as his mouth settled into a grim line, his face momentarily melancholy.

"But you've never come close to love, yourself?"

He made a face as he struggled with his answer. "Honestly? Yes. I've come close." Slowly, he raised somber eyes to connect with hers. "At least five times."

She smiled at this wan joke and then was puzzled when his expression remained serious. "You fell in love with one of them." She attacked abruptly and knew she'd hit the mark when she saw the shielded pain that flickered in his eyes. "You fell in love with one of your students."

He stood suddenly, shaking his head and running both hands back through the sleek black of his hair.

"What happened to her?"

Her mentor shrugged as he turned away. "She bailed out of the project and went back…to her former life."

"She loved you too," Kansas whispered to herself. She frowned as she considered his back. "Do you ever see her? Talk to her?"

His back remained turned as he shook his head. "No. That wouldn't be fair."

"And she's never tried to reach you?"

"No."

"She loved you too much to take another mate? But not enough to try to see you again?"

"She wouldn't know where to find me. Just like you won't know where to find me, when you leave here. You were unconscious when they brought you here." Turning back to face her, he seemed to struggle to put a small smile on his face. "But, that was a long time ago," he said as he let his eyes travel over her nude body. "You're tired," he stated, "I'll let you sleep."

"Where will *you* sleep?"

"Beside you, once you've nodded off. You won't even know I'm there. Shall I cover you with the blankets?"

"No," she told him. "It feels good like this."

He nodded without surprise, letting his eyes slide down her body and rest warmly in the brown thatch of hair between her legs, then threw himself into the chair.

Chapter Five

ཐ

At some point in the night, Kansas woke on her back, restless as the result of strange, evocative dreams. As she shifted, trying to rearrange herself on the bed, she felt the weight of a strong arm banding her midriff. Cracking her eyes open, she found her instructor asleep beside her, his rugged, curving lips inches from her own. "Don't struggle, Kansas," he muttered in a voice heavy with sleep.

He knew her name.

Startled by this idea, Kansas lay awake waiting for morning, watching the darkly handsome face on the pillow beside hers. His long face was beautifully vital and alive even in sleep, somehow sweeter with his driven nature in remission and without the dark flashes of panic haunting his eyes. His forehead was smooth and untroubled, his black eyebrows at peace as his thick, black, spiking eyelashes fluttered through some pleasing dream. As she watched, the corner of his mouth tightened into several short quick smiles and he muttered his way through a brief sequence of words, some of which included "always", "never" and "love".

As she watched the man's strong, handsome features, strange, novel feelings were swirling in places she'd never taken much note of before. In her chest near the tips of her nipples, between her legs deep inside her womb, and at the base of her spine there evolved a strange liquid weakness that spread into the top of her thighs and stroked the back of her knees. As the unexpected longings gripped her body, she stared at the man beside her, knowing the longings had something to do with him—that they probably had a *lot* to do with him—and that they probably had a lot to do with sex as well. And somehow she knew that only he could help dispel the strange disquiet and gnawing hunger that had started a slow burn between her legs.

She stared at his face with sudden understanding, realizing how a starstruck student might easily become addicted to him, suspecting that a woman could become dependent on *this man* even more than the eroticism and sex he would make her a slave to.

Without consciously admitting to it, she wanted the man and his touch. Recalling the faint, intoxicating tingle she'd experienced during their brief contact of the day before, and wondering how he would feel pressed up against her today, she reached out to him, straining to reach him, wanting only to get the feel of him on her fingertips. Failing in that attempt because of the straps binding her to the headboard, she bowed her body into an arch and maneuvered her face toward his, using her lips to brush the stubbled curve of his chin in a last-ditch effort to take in and absorb some of the texture of that rough, masculine jaw.

Stretching herself to her limit, she tried to put her lips on his without much success, though her nipples did manage to reach out and capture a bit of soft jersey at their tips as she pressed up against his T-shirt. Intent on her task, her eyes on his lips, it was a few seconds before she realized he was awake and watching her from beneath lowered eyelids. Breathlessly, she stared into the heat of his blue gaze while he slowly tilted his head and placed his mouth over hers.

Pleasant didn't begin to describe the sensation that sprang to life and swamped her senses as her lips came into warm contact with the rough silk of his. Rubbing his mouth over hers with I'm-not-taking-no-for-an-answer insistence, his lips prodded and pushed and pressured hers while he grasped her upper arms in his big hands and stretched her body out then rolled on top of her. Everything was happening at once and all of it was insanely delicious. His lips were rough and demanding, his grip tight and controlling as his knee forged a place between her thighs, urging them to part, and the thick bulge of his cock crushed into her lower belly. His tongue was in her mouth, hot and invasive, temperamental and eager, as he pulled his hips upward to rub the imposing ridge of his canvas-clad shaft into her belly.

Panting with effort and growing excitement, Kansas lay caught beneath his weight, straining her neck to receive his tongue more deeply, bowing her back in an instinctive attempt to put her breasts up against his chest. At the same time, the coarse canvas stretching over his cock was burning a line into her tender flesh as he continued to drive his lower body against hers, the action a ruthless male demand for more. Kansas gasped into his mouth and her sobbing intake was followed by his own groaning rumble—the sound wrenched from deep within his chest to work its way up his throat and hang on wet lips and open mouth.

And Kansas recognized that this wasn't handbook stuff he was doing to her. This wasn't even instructor stuff. In fact, this wasn't even for her.

This was for him.

Despite his handbook and his determination to follow its maxims, despite his best-laid plans and his intention to adhere to them, despite his claims at a cool and indifferent professionalism, her mentor's resolve was crumpling beneath an elemental and primal need he could neither deny nor control as he yielded to an overpoweringly masculine need to dominate and take and have…more.

This aggressive, undeniable display of male need stirred a reciprocal female interest within her own body, aching and burning and twisting her insides with a wanton desire to have this man against her—his flesh against hers, his body using hers to satisfy his own need—as well as to address the novel yearnings and hungers that stirred to life within her.

Tentatively, she pushed her body up to meet his. The thick, heavy ridge in his groin dragged at her flesh as he pushed into her belly again and Kansas whimpered at the coarse, abrasive contact of the rough fabric grazing and scorching her skin with every scraping pass. Catching back a whimper of discomfort, she tried to reposition herself beneath his laboring thrusts when he stopped suddenly, dragged his lips from hers, and stared at her, his breath ragged and uneven.

"I'm hurting you," he groaned, his eyes closing in realization, then opening again to gaze hungrily into hers. "I'm sorry."

Wonderingly, still not understanding, she gazed up at the fire in his eyes, at the purpose, the drive. Her eyes dropped to his curving mouth—open and spilling warm hurried breaths onto her lips.

Stunned, she stared at him. Here was a man with purpose. A man who *lived* for…something. The other men she knew—the men she worked with and shared a cube with—were content, but they lived their lives without purpose.

"You…need this…sex…don't you?"

Again his eyes closed an instant as his lips twisted. "It's just that I have a lot to accomplish today and…I'm so on edge. I don't want to do something wrong."

"Something wrong?"

"I have to follow the handbook but I don't know if I can. Feeling like this. So hot. So close. So fucking on *edge*—like I'm burning alive."

She nodded as she writhed internally, moved by the tightly contained passion and honest vulnerability revealed in his coarse words at the same time that she was aroused by his pantingly hot male presence. His chest crushed into hers with every long rasping breath he sucked into his lungs while his half-closed eyes rested on her mouth, his gaze avaricious and intent.

"On the second day, you're only supposed to touch me," she whispered.

His eyebrows moved together as he nodded painfully.

"So touch me," she whispered in a faintly shaking voice. "Touch me all over and take what you need."

"Fuck," he growled in a low, needy sound of suppressed darkness. His eyes narrowed on hers as he forced out a short bark of laughter. "This isn't going to work," he told her, hanging his head and shaking it. Breathlessly, she watched his dark hair toss as it slid across his face.

She answered his growl with her own low moan. "We'll make it work," she insisted. "I'll help you." Hard, heavy breaths were racking her lungs as she lowered her gaze to search between their bodies. "Please. Touch me. Touch me with…your cock. Let me feel it on my skin. Let me feel it on my breasts, on my face. Touch my lips. Use me, mentor. Use me to satisfy your need," she begged in a whisper, recognizing how far she had fallen with the utterance of those words, and that want. How far she had fallen from her lofty aim to escape the Anomaly Category of society.

Closing his eyes again, he rumbled another groan that was heavy with need.

"The handbook has strictly stated rules for you to follow?"

"Yes," he bit back, opening his eyes and glaring down at her.

"But there are none for me," she stated, somehow knowing that was true. Briefly, she considered how easily she had fallen off the wagon of "normal behavior". Fallen without a bounce. Then she plunged ahead. "What would happen if I wrapped my hand around your cock...while you were thrusting against me?"

When his eyes widened at the mere thought, she smiled.

"I knew this was going to happen," he complained with a moan. With shaking hands, he ripped his slacks open and got them off, then stripped his T-shirt over his head. Getting onto his knees, he straddled her hips, his cock in his hand as he moved up her body, stopping when his knees were wedged beneath her armpits.

When he rested back on his heels, she felt the warm weight of his scrotum resting below her breasts and watched his fist stroke roughly up the long shaft of his cock, the length flushed and wrapped in a bold network of dark veins. When he leaned forward, his balls swung to graze the sensitive skin of her breasts as he touched the fat, silken head of his dark cock to her lips.

Pressing her lips against the bruised color of his full cock head, she placed a soft kiss on the slit nestled into the crown and then watched a silvery drop of his release well from the small open slash. She heard him suck in a breath and whisper a curse. Then one of his large hands curled behind her head to grip the back of her skull as he turned her face and rubbed his long length against her cheek, his testes rough-soft where they brushed her chin.

The fragile skin of his steel-hard erection was silky smooth as it caressed her cheek and all the raw, masculine power of his narrow hips was nudged up close to her face, within kissing distance. She could feel his heat captured and held in the damp, humid curls that gathered in his groin. Acting on impulse, she angled her head to press her lips into the tautly stretched skin of his groin where the thick root of his cock sprang out of tangled dark curls. "Fuck," he gasped, and with a firm hand on the back of her skull he held her kiss into his crotch, his hips rolling as he rubbed his erection against the side of her face. When he finally pulled away, his eyes were alight with a mixture of feral heat and burning pleasure. "Now watch me," he told her in a raw, edgy voice. "Just watch me and it will be enough."

Resting on his heels, he straddled her midriff and she watched his large hand wrapped around the thick length of his shaft, stroking and pulling at the tight skin as his fist moved up and down the heavy rod of flesh. His legs were spread in an indecent carnal pose as he worked his hand over his cock—dark and vein-rich—and her eyes flicked to his face where his teeth were wedged in his bottom lip. As his eyes closed, he choked back a strangled grunt and she returned her gaze to his cock, watching it jerk in his pistoning fist, spurting thick ejaculate as he levered his shaft downward and spilled out onto her breasts.

"Lord of the Republic," he whispered hoarsely as his eyes opened and he watched himself surge out onto her skin. For several moments he stared, his eyes lost in a deep, hypnotic trance, then he used the dark flesh in his hand to spread his cum over her breasts and paint her nipples with his glistening release.

* * * * *

"Don't tie me," she requested when she'd returned from the facility. He looked down at her as he considered her request. He didn't want to tie her. He wanted her hands on him, her arms around him, holding him—not fighting him. "I don't want you fighting me," he eventually told her. "I have a lot to accomplish today."

"I won't fight you," she told him quickly, convincingly. "I *want* you...to touch me. With your hands. With your lips."

For a few heartbeats he was silent as his eyes burned and his throat worked. "Take those white panties off," he finally growled.

Swiftly, she pushed them down her legs, stepping out of them when they reached the floor.

The next thing she knew, she was on her back on the bed and his hands were all over her. And it felt so good. Just the warm contact of another human body—a warm, living, very male body pressed up against hers—his hands moving to grope and grasp at every curve on her body.

She reveled in it, stretched instinctively, arched within the tight circle of his arms and felt his lips graze across the nipple of one breast—hurried and eager as his wide hand plunged between her legs. "Open your legs," he commanded as his lips moved up to tease the corner of her mouth. She watched his gaze lower to her thighs as she separated them for the warm hand holding her mound. "Wider," he ordered and she complied, watching him smile with a tight, hard breath.

With his face close to hers and his heated gaze on his hand in the curls at her mound, she felt her labia part beneath an exploratory finger at the same time that he sighed with rough satisfaction and dragged his finger through the moist folds between her legs.

"I'm going to play with you," he warned her with a rough-edged voice. "I'm going to play with your sex until you're wet. After that, we'll have to be careful. I don't want to go too far," he told her. "Don't let me go too far," he whispered.

"I won't let you," she gasped back at him as his finger settled on what felt like the very center of her need.

Lightly, his finger touched that same point with tantalizing, brushing contact, nudging her toward a madness of unfulfilled need. Anxiously, wanting to cry out, wanting something she couldn't name, she shifted beneath him and he laughed breathlessly, his gaze still on his hand between her legs. "That's right, open your legs, December. Bring your knees up."

In answer, she slid her feet up the bed's surface, spreading her legs wider at the same time. "Oh, Lord," she complained in a whisper, "I want… I want…"

"More?" he suggested. And with this word, two of his fingers captured the needy bit of flesh in a gentle clamp. His fingertips were either side of the tight knot of pleasure that burned between her legs, working it with random movement that brought about a very purposeful result. "Oh, Lord," she sobbed out, stiff with anticipation, not wanting to move. Not wanting to chance any action that might interrupt the pleasure he was delivering to her open sex.

Despite this fact, she found herself twisting beneath his hand as her knees dropped slightly toward the bed and the line of her sex opened even wider, begging shamelessly for the rapacious sweep of his fingers. Begging for his strafing touch. Beseeching him to manhandle the tender, fragile stuff between her legs that made her a woman.

"That's right," he told her in a raw, uneven voice. "Move for me, December."

She groaned as she twisted. "How?"

"Roll your hips," he rasped breathlessly. "Roll your hips and pump your pussy up into my hand. Spread your legs, plant your feet and pump yourself against me."

She wanted to cry helplessly, scream wantonly and shout a demand for more. She wanted more from him. But when she started moving, her body seemed to know what to do. Her bottom lifted from the bed and rocked up to meet his glorious, gifted hand as the pure pleasure blazing between her legs increased unbearably.

His breath was hot and damp against her cheek and she watched him swallow hungrily, his blue gaze riveted on her pumping hips.

All at once there were a lot of fingers sliding inside her slippery sex and he stopped with a panting groan, the heel of his palm resting on her mound.

"Don't…stop," she whimpered, pushing her sex into his large, warm hand, pleading for any comfort he could offer her.

"Have to," he panted on a ragged breath. "You're too close."

"It feels…so good," she whimpered painfully and he smiled down on her. "I know," he murmured. "Believe me. I know." He touched her lips with his then worked his way down her body, pulling his lips and his warm breath over her skin as he made his way toward her belly button, sank his tongue into the soft cup and picked up an erotic rhythm as he held her hips and thrust his tongue hard and deep at the giving flesh surrounding the deep dimple on her stomach. She heard a deep, warm, restless giggle of pleasure and realized the breathless laughter was hers, spilling from her lips in soft murmurs.

"You like that?" he whispered roughly, lifting his head, his eyes burning into hers. "You like my tongue in your belly?"

She nodded.

"Well, if you liked my tongue in your belly button," he rasped in a low, warm voice, "you're going to love my cock in your pussy."

Immediately, he moved lower, sliding down her body and pushing her legs wider as he pulled her labia apart with his fingers and gazed, spellbound, at her open sex. She felt his gaze as though he had touched her and the length of her vagina blinked an instant then opened greedily. His throat worked as he swallowed hard. "Fuck," he whispered. "You're so wet," he murmured. "I'd love to drag a finger up through your folds to test you but I think you're too close. This is the part where you have to help. Give me your hands." Taking her hands, he guided them between her legs as he rested one of his large palms over her fingers and massaged the sodden lips of her sex. "This is where you have to take over," he told her. "Just do to yourself what I was doing before.

"No. Not like that. Get your fingers inside your lips. Open your labia for me, darling. That's right. That's beautiful." Reaching out, he guided one of her fingers to a little knot of flesh high on the line of her soft, wet sex. "Now play with yourself, December. Play yourself right into orgasm." Avidly, hungrily, he watched her open sex while she stroked at the needy little center. "Hurry," he whispered, his hand wrapped around his thickening cock, stroking slowly. "Hurry, December. It's all I can do to keep my dick in my fist instead of balls deep inside you. Hurry."

Restlessly, she licked her lips as she watched his eyes—fixed between her legs.

Feeling lost and uncertain about where she was going and how she was getting there, she yearned for him in a way she didn't understand. On some deep level, she knew that this—all of this—all that she was feeling, was because of him. The very female need clawing at her sanity was in some way connected to him, centered on him. And all at once she was certain she couldn't do this without him—that, if she did, it would somehow be empty and useless. She wanted his touch.

Wanted his fingers in her pussy.

Wanted him doing it to her.

"Help me," she whispered, her fingers suddenly still, her head tossing as she shook it in refusal. "Help me, mentor. I want you. I want you to do this to me. Please."

She heard him snarl.

With a guttered wrench of male anguish he was on top of her, his cock head at the mouth of her sex as he spread her legs and prepared to mount her. His eyes were wild and feral and he grunted as he held the root of his cock, the broad tip pressing against the mouth of her sex.

Then some light came into his eyes and he jerked himself away.

Throwing himself across the room, he dragged his black slacks up his legs, pushed his feet into a pair of slip-ons and grabbed up a long coat as he pushed through the door and slammed it behind him.

Chapter Six

ꙮ

Thankfully, the day was cold and vicious. Slashing rain beat down at Hardin and gave him an excuse to pull his collar up, hiding his angry face as he hunched his shoulders and strode through the storm-washed streets. Few people were out in the mean weather on the normally crowded sidewalks. No one heard him flog himself with coarse words and cruel adjectives, muttered through clenched teeth as he stalked the streets broodingly, his hands shoved deep inside the pockets of his coat.

He stopped as his head dropped back in frustration, almost screaming into the rain-drenched air. "Why can't she understand?" he shouted at the dark, miserable sky. A couple of attractive young women hurried by, averting eyes that didn't understand and never would.

"Anomaly," the first woman noted without emotion. "Waste of breathable air," she continued blandly, and her companion nodded, her eyes downcast, watching for the puddles in the street.

Defeated, exhausted, Hardin felt his shoulders slump as he turned to watch the cold women pick their way through the rain-chilled streets. Flicking his head to move black strands of wet hair away from his eyes, he shivered as he reached inside his coat to adjust the aching flesh that threatened to breach his fly. Turning slowly, he took the first few steps that would carry him back to the warmth of his cube, to the warmth of the woman waiting there, to the warmth of December.

* * * * *

When Hardin walked through the door, she was sitting on the edge of the bed. In her hand was a pair of faded blue panties. "These are mine," she told him.

Shrugging his coat down his arms, he shook it out and hung it on the peg beside the door. Crossing the room on his way to his kitchen-eat, he nodded.

"I lost them four years ago. I…paid a lot for them. For the off-standard size…and the color. They were a…brilliant blue."

Reaching into a cupboard for a heavy glass tumbler, Hardin splashed out a drink from an unmarked bottle. "Electric blue," he grunted. "But they've been washed a few times since then."

"I lost them four years ago," she insisted.

He drank off the inch of liquor before he answered. "Five," he corrected her.

"Five?"

"You lost them five years ago."

"But…how could that be?"

She jumped when he slammed the glass back down on the counter.

"Because that's how long I've been in love with you!"

"Wh-at?"

Leaning over to reach the far side of the counter, he punched a series of buttons and Kansas watched, stunned, as a sequence of visuals popped up to hover above the aluminum coffee table. Each one documented two lovers energetically engaged in sex, their bodies pumping against each other in various poses. Kansas stared at one of the couples, their bodies overlain with a sheen of sweat, the man between the woman's legs, the thick root of his cock glimmering with moisture each time he pulled back, just before he punched into her again.

"That's us!" she blurted in startled realization, amazed at the bliss on the face of her own image—and shocked at the intensity with which the man drove into her.

"That's us," he said in a low voice. "That's five…four years of us."

She looked at him, horror-stricken.

He blew out a breath. "At the end of your training, you'll be given the option to continue with the project. To pick a mate and continue. If you refuse, you'll be permitted to return to your previous life. Your memory will be wiped clean. You'll wake up—"

"In a clinic," she finished for him.

"They'll tell you you're suffering from exhaustion or that you're—"

"Subject to fits and memory loss."

Accepting this information, he nodded. "You were my best student," he said quietly. "My best student ever. The first time I slid my hand between your legs you were wet…and I hadn't done anything more than look at you.

"I'm sorry," he said in a gravelly voice of sincerity and she wondered at the man who'd been forced to make this apology at least four times previously. "I'm sorry. I just can't…accept the fact that I've failed you. You of all people," he whispered in a falling voice. "Once a year, Davis—my employer—lets me have another chance. She gives *us* another chance. And every year when we get together I'm determined to follow the handbook. But the moment I see you, the fucking handbook goes right out the virtual window, along with all my common sense and control. And every year I end up inside you, sharing your first orgasm.

And every year you make the same decision. You go back to cubelife.

"Please, Kansas. Don't let me fail this time. This segment of the project is coming to a close. This is your *last* chance. Next year you'll be considered too old by one year. This is your last chance at a life. A real life! A life like our ancestors lived, full of passion and laughter and purpose!

"Don't let me fail," he scraped out in a voice of desperation.

She blinked as she stared at him. "Have I seen these…documents before? Have you shown them to me?"

He shook his head. "This is the first time you've seen them. This time I'm desperate, Kansas."

Slowly, her fascinated gaze returned to the lovers on the table.

She had never thought herself beautiful. But the woman on the table *was* beautiful, her head thrown back, her eyes half-closed, her eyebrows arched, her lips parted and panting. Her mentor stood behind her, one arm wrapped around her midriff, his fingers sprawled over a breast while the other held her chin with infinite tenderness. His lips nestled against the side of her neck and her head tilted as a small, warm smile appeared at the edges of her mouth.

Kansas stared at his image, making love to hers. "I'm sorry," she told him in a whisper. "I'm sorry I've put you through this. But I want you to do that to me. I want you to make me beautiful."

He groaned in answer, his fists knotted at his sides as he moved around the counter toward her, the lines of his body tightening with barely controlled passion. "Beautiful?" he choked out through gritted teeth. "But you *are* beautiful. Beautiful, exotic and rare. I *won't* fuck this up again," he spat out the six hard words. "No, Kansas! Every December for four years I've fought my attraction to you…and failed."

She shook her head. "Then don't fight it," she told him. "This will be our last week together?"

He nodded.

"Let me give you this week. In return for all you've done for me. In return for all you've tried to do for me." She took a breath deep into her lungs. "What if I promised to choose a mate at the end of our week together? Couldn't we just ignore the handbook? What difference would it make?"

"Maybe," he allowed, his eyes shifting restlessly among the several visuals playing on the table then finally returning to gaze at her. "Maybe…except for this first step."

She held his gaze. "Then I'll do it. I'll do this. And at the end of the week I'll choose a mate."

"You promise to continue with the program? That you'll mate and have children?"

"I promise," she told him solemnly, nodding her head. "What about you? What will *you* do afterward?"

"I have a plan," he answered.

"That doesn't include me?"

"That doesn't include you," he told her, his voice edged with determination.

She stared at him. "Tell me your name," she demanded quietly. "You know my name. Tell me yours."

Moving across the room, he backed away from her until he came up against the edge of his dressing case. With white knuckles he grasped the edge of the case, clutching it in his fierce grip. "Put the blue panties on," he commanded hoarsely, then watched intently as she pulled the faded fabric up her legs. "Now sit on the edge of the bed and spread your legs again. Pull your lips open. No," he corrected her immediately. "Put your hands inside your panties. Yes," he breathed. "Like that. Now edge the top of your panties down a bit so I can see your hands in your pussy. That's it, December.

"It's Hardin," he told her with a raw, unsteady voice. "My name is Hardin." Then he watched, heart hammering, as she played the line of her sex, her eyes on his, keening his name as she hurried herself forward and climaxed under her own hand. As he watched, his fingers worked almost without his knowledge, pulling his fly open and starting his slacks on their way to the floor.

Like a drunk, he staggered toward her, fell to his knees on the ground before her and wrenched her legs wide as he reached for her with greedy pawing hands, his fingers dragging in the hot wet crotch of her silk panties. Then his mouth was on the comfortingly familiar fabric, eating into her sex which burned behind the frail, stretched barrier as his tongue licked at the silky stuff and prodded at her soft, tender opening. Briefly lifting his mouth out of her crotch, Hardin pulled the top of the panties down far enough to get his lips sucked up against her pink, plump labia. His lips moved fervently over her sex as he dragged the dampened panties lower in order to reach her, to improve his access and pull his tongue down through her heated, wet sex and into her pulsing vagina.

"Just a taste," he murmured into her flooding pussy. "Just a taste," he insisted as his hands clamped her hips and he put a long, hungry French kiss into her slit, hardly even aware that she was coming again. Her thighs trembled, her cunt spasmed and her hips bucked in his clenching grasp as he lashed her sex with his tongue and then gentled her with the warm press of his open lips.

Finally, he broke from her, gasping, as he threw himself on the bed and pulled her up to join him. He stretched his body out behind hers and dragged her leg up over his thigh with a rough, demanding urgency, spreading her wide as he lifted his knee inside hers. Shaking with a terrible, compelling need, his hand slipped into the front of her panties and fingered her wet folds cavalierly as he prodded his cock head at the damp well between her legs. The dark, slitted head of his cock pushed against the fragile fabric that barred his entrance into her cunt, the silk now slick with her moisture as well as his own dribbling wash of pre-cum. His cock burned as he shoved his rod along the silk several times and then came between her legs, surging as he emptied all over her faded blue panties.

Stunned with lust, he felt himself thicken again as he raised his upper body with one arm, ran his fingers into the puddle of shining semen and spread it to coat the worn silk that stretched across her mound. In a daze, he got his hand into the front of her panties and pulled them back, watching as he settled three thick fingers over her vulva and started a slow pumping action against the sensitized rim of her opening, allowing her need to rebuild in hungry stages, watching her clit shiver each time he plunged his fingers into her vagina and pulled on the line of her pussy. Again, she came, her cunt clasping on his fingers in a series of shuddering swallows as he shot his middle finger deep and held her entire clenching sex in his hand. As she climaxed, he pressured the long line of her sex into never-ending orgasm as he nudged a continuing, surging response from her. Just when she thought she was finished, he tightened his hold again, dragging another satisfying contraction out of her cunt with the hard grip of his hand wrapping her sex.

"Is it…always like this?" she gasped, staring at him with stunned awe.

His gave her a warm smile. "You're special," he told her, "although a good mentor can milk an awful lot of pleasure out of a single orgasm. Draw it out. Make it last with a bit of pressure in the right place at the right time, coaxing out those last shuddering convulsions."

His fingers tightened to clamp on her pussy again and he felt her body clench again—a small lingering tribute to ecstasy.

"And it gets better…when I get inside you. When I hit your dark spot."

"My dark spot?"

He nodded as he pulled her panties down her legs and off over her feet. "Right at the back of your cunt. There's a spot that longs to be stroked, taken, beaten…fucked," he murmured, settling back on the bed, collecting her into his arms and breathing against her ear. "And it can only be reached by a man. It can only be reached…with my cock."

Wide-eyed, she turned her head to stare back at him. "I'm going to fall in love with you again," she told him with great certainty. "Probably today."

His eyes closed then opened again. "I know," he told her, smearing his lips into her temple, "but I've got five days to change your mind."

"How," she asked him, "do you plan to do that?"

He gave her a wry smile. "Fuck you silly from now through the end of the week?"

"And you expect that to work?"

He shrugged. "Not really."

She gave him a soft, tender smile. "Well, then, let's get started."

"I was hoping you'd say that," he told her as he rolled on top of her.

"What should I do?" she asked, uncertain but eager.

His eyes closed as he considered every sinful demand he could make of her, knowing she'd deliver. "Just do whatever comes naturally," he whispered, loving her spontaneity in bed, wanting her to surprise him as she had so many times in the past, with some intimately erotic act that he hadn't suggested, that he hadn't choreographed and directed.

As he lay between her legs, his cock head nudging her wet entrance, she brought her knees up beside him and opened her legs wide.

"Oh, yes," he breathed. "That will work...for starters."

Then he was inside her—finally—and he had to suck in a breath, blinking hard as her vagina compressed the long, hard length of his shaft. She shifted beneath his weight as her vagina closed around him like a velvet glove. "Isn't it...supposed to hurt the first time?" she queried hesitantly.

He smiled at her lovingly. "It did...the first time," he told her. "But that was five years ago."

"Are you...documenting this?" she asked almost shyly.

He nodded as he pulled his hips and stretched into her again.

"Play the visual for me," she breathed. "Life-sized. I want to watch you do this to me."

He stopped and stared at her, then ran his hand into her hair at her temple. "You're amazing," he told her in a voice roughened with emotion...and anticipation.

* * * * *

Hardin left her long enough to punch some buttons on the countertop. Then, with their visual images rotating above the table beside the bed and with his massive cock fully sheathed inside her, Kansas felt his mouth, hot and hungry on her breast as he suckled and dragged on her nipple with tongue and teeth and lips. He worked her over so fiercely that she felt it like a tug of wanton pleasure at the back of her vagina where his cock stretched and filled and hammered with a promise of fulfilling violence that was deeply provoking and wonderfully satisfying. She couldn't help the instinctual need to open her legs obscenely wide and cant her hips slightly so she could take him at the very back of her cunt where her need was greatest. The lips of her sex spread open beneath his plowing groin and she whispered in pleasure with each delicious drag of his hot, demanding flesh against her open labia. As he moved on her, she pushed her wet, needy pussy into his groin and reveled in the pleasure of his damp skin dragging at her labia, exciting her clit, while the huge width of his shaft stretched the rim of her vulva beyond bearing and his cock head pounded against her womb.

Feeling sinful and deliciously dirty, she watched the visual, watched him fucking her, watched the dark wet hair curled at his groin, the thick root of his cock stretching her open as he pulled and slammed and pulled again, his testes swinging to meet her bottom as he banged into her.

Dragging her eyes away from their pumping images, she returned her gaze to his face, hanging over hers—a dark ripped snarl on his silent lips, black hair hanging in damp strands and shadowing his forehead as his eyes narrowed with every savage thrust of his hips.

There was a fine, glimmering sheen of sweat on the smooth muscles ripping his chest as he moved over her, and each breath he pulled in was a rasping gasp of raw pleasure and an obvious struggle to prolong this wet, sliding, provoking bliss. Inside her body, her vagina was subjected to an aching madness that built with each hard cramming thrust of his cock and she pushed her legs wider again, waiting and wanting—and wanting to wait—to pull this moment of near consummation into eternity. The pleasure building inside her was deep and wickedly carnal and intimated a dark, complete satisfaction to follow. In her mad, heady need, she murmured, and he slowed, his shaft seated at the back of her cunt, his cock pulsing fiercely.

"*What?*" he whispered hoarsely. "What did you say?"

She blinked up at him and shook her head, suddenly reluctant to repeat the words she hadn't meant for him to hear. "You're beautiful too," she finally said, "when you're fucking me like this."

His neck arched forward spilling his dark hair onto her face and she felt a surge thicken his cock as a series of guttural snarls almost choked him. Then his lips crushed down onto hers and he fucked her mouth with his tongue at the same time that his hips drove against her and she screamed into his mouth—screamed in long, never-ending, cunt-quenching climax.

When they woke together later, they lay wrapped around each other on the bed, Kansas on her back, gazing at the window high on the wall. Together they watched the stars inch across the sky, dragging the moon's arc of light diagonally across the dark rectangle of glass. "Have you ever been to the moon?" she queried languidly.

He nodded into her neck, where his lips were sealed against her skin. "On a school trip when I was eighteen. Why?"

"What was it like?"

He shrugged. "At the time, I was more interested in my teacher, Ms. VanderKoven." There was a moment's silence before this statement was explained. "It occurred to me at an early age that there was something wrong with me. Something seriously wrong. Every now and again my cock would get hard. I didn't know what the hell was going on...but I knew it had something to do with women." Again he shrugged. "I kept it to myself and pumped myself out whenever I could get a private moment.

"I started drinking when I was young. Black-market stuff." He laughed. "I was a mess about eight years ago—fasting for days to enhance the pleasure administered by my own hand. I was down to one-hundred-eighty pounds when I got drunk and ended up on a shuttle to Beta 4." He nodded at her wide-eyed expression. "Yeah. Our most distant satellite outpost. Two weeks out and two weeks back. Slept all the way there *and* all the way back. The passengers are put into stasis during the transfer. But I don't even remember arriving at the satellite station. I woke up at the station back here on earth, in an office full of very angry government officials. Evidently I'd boarded the shuttle without ticketcard or passport. They were pissed.

"*And* I lost my job after an unexplained absence of four weeks."

"I'm sorry."

He shook his head. "As it turned out, this job came up at about the same time. It probably saved my life. And, for the next three years…and thirty-six women," she felt his smile, "I was happy. Then I met you." He nuzzled his lips against the side of her neck, sucking slightly and putting a tiny bite of pain on the skin beneath his mouth. "After that, I wanted more." He blew out a sigh. "But my sperm count is nil. I'm ineligible as a mate candidate."

"What are you going to do…at the end of this week?"

"Go on a bender," he laughed quietly. "A Beta 4 bender."

"And after that?"

"And after that," he sighed, "I'll go back to work." He rolled onto her. "But, between now and then I'm going to fuck you…oh…at least thirty-two different ways and at least fifty-two separate times."

She laughed. "At the risk of repeating yourself," she teased.

"At the risk of repeating myself," he confirmed. "But some of the positions are so good, they bear repeating."

"Oh?" she encouraged him, "which ones specifically?"

He closed his eyes as he considered his answer. There was a great deal of contentment in his expression and her heart softened to see him…happy.

Clearing his throat he answered her as he opened his eyes. "My cock in your mouth. My cock in your mouth. And…my cock in your mouth."

"Three times?"

"At least three times…before the end of the week."

Chapter Seven

Six days later, Hardin was sitting in his supervisor's office. Davis had rearranged her plans in order to work him into her schedule. Hardin had made an unusual request.

"You're sure about this," Davis asked the man seated before her. Resolutely, Hardin nodded back as Davis considered the face that belonged to her best agent.

He was still the most handsome man she'd ever seen, even in a population full of perfect men. His dark good looks were slightly exotic, just faintly…anomalous. His eyes were stunningly blue against his brown skin. Today those eyes were troubled, and tired smudges curved beneath his lower lashes, but his face was determined.

"You're asking me to erase five years of your life. That's a lot different than losing a month, Hardin. Most people can shake a month off and return to their previous lives—everything still familiar. But you're an intelligent man, Hardin. You'll ask questions. You might spend the rest of your life just trying to get those years back, trying to rediscover your past."

"I was with the program five years ago, before I met Kansas, so I'll have some basis of familiarity—something to go back to," he insisted stubbornly.

Davis stared at him for several moments. "If you're certain, then."

With his eyes on the ground, Hardin gave a determined nod.

"And you're doing this because?"

"I love her. I can't live—I prefer not to live knowing I'll never be with her." He cleared his throat. "I want you to do me a favor." Digging into the front pocket of his canvas slacks, he produced a bit of worn blue silk. For a few seconds, he stared at the silk in his hand before he placed the panties on the desk.

"If," he said, "I ever come to you, years from now, wondering what the fuck my life is worth, I want you to show me these. And tell me the story that goes with them."

"Oh geez, Hardin," Davis choked out as she pushed her chair back and opened her desk drawer. Pulling out a plastic card, she ran her palmwand over it and pushed it toward him.

"Will you do that for me?" he asked her. But Davis just pointed at the card in answer.

Reaching for the card, he thanked her then stopped as his eyes caught on the orders printed on the card's surface. His gaze narrowed on the card uncertainly, then cut to hers questioningly as he shook his head.

Davis stood and turned quickly to walk across the room. There she stopped, facing the wall and wiping at her eyes before she turned again and leaned to sit against the edge of a starkly white counter, fixing her eyes on her long legs crossed at the ankles. "Let me tell you a story," she told him in an unsteady voice.

"The story starts about eight years ago in the early years of the program. We located a very promising male prospect—a very fertile male. We discovered him while trawling the black market. That's where we come by a lot of our prospects. You didn't know that," she stated and shrugged apologetically. "The most promising prospects are already discontent and showing signs of it, looking for black-market books, trying to buy alcohol or drugs…or sex.

"We had high hopes for the man. He was recruited and trained by our very best. All that remained was for him to choose a mate. The days passed. Three weeks passed! He flirted, romanced and screwed with every young female prospect in the program but wouldn't settle down. He was creating havoc as one after another of our girls fell for him and then had trouble moving on. We needed couples, Hardin. Couples who could start new families, raise children. He was dropped from the program."

Eyes narrowed, Hardin shook his head at his supervisor.

"Then we started all over. Considering him a *hopeless case*," she smiled wryly, "at least where love was concerned—but recognizing his potential—we erased his memory and recruited him as an instructor."

Hardin's eyes widened as his jaw dropped.

Davis nodded. "You."

Slowly he shook his head as he stared at his supervisor. "I never lost my memory," he countered, uncomprehendingly.

She gave him a questioning smile in answer. "No?"

He blinked a few times as his eyes focused on the floor. "The shuttle to Beta 4," he said with slow realization. "I lost a month traveling to the satellite outpost."

Davis just continued to smile. "You were never on the shuttle to Beta 4."

His gaze swept up from the floor to burn at her accusingly. "That...was a dirty trick," he declared.

She agreed with a guilty nod. Her eyes glowed happily as her smile widened.

He stood suddenly. "But...why? Why have you let this go on for *years*? Knowing how I felt about Kansas? From the start! Or, at least, almost from the start!"

She shrugged. "You're our best agent." Taking in his expression of disgust, she followed this with a sigh and a grimace. "I've been doing my best, Hardin. I could have given her another instructor. I *would* have, except for the fact that you're a fertile male! I've been working on your behalf for the last five years. But I have supervisors too. They didn't believe me when I told them this was the real thing. One week! What's one week with one woman? They wanted to see some sort of a commitment out of you before they tried to make a mate out of you, again. To put it bluntly, we can't *use* the sort of man who would cheat on his wife and cause chaos at the base. My supervisors wanted proof that it would last." She nodded at the card on her desk. "That card will get you on the next outbound lift to the Seychelles."

He stood abruptly, his eyes wild with hope, flicking at the door then back to his employer.

"Room Ten," she told him, then continued as he turned for the door. "And you might like to know that she kept her promise. She's waiting in there for her first mate candidate, though she doesn't appear to be very happy about it."

He turned to face her again. "Thank you, Davis," he said fervently and took a few quick steps toward her. Grabbing her around the waist he planted a long, loving kiss on her mouth, dragging a hand through the gray streak in her hair. "Thanks," he repeated, smiling at her a single breathless moment. "And it might interest *you* to know," he winked as he slid the blue panties off the desk and backed across the room, "that you would have been my second choice."

With that, he stuffed the blue silk back into his pocket as he strode through the door.

Davis smiled, a mixture of pure pleased amusement and wry longing as she nodded her head at the closed door. "Thanks," she murmured to herself, her fingers on her lips. Sighing, she moved across the room and dropped into her chair, still staring at the door. "Thanks, Hardin. That absolutely frickin' makes my day."

* * * * *

She had her back to the door when it opened. Standing at the virtual window, Kansas stared into it without seeing. She didn't notice the cloudy sky crack open as the sun spilled through the gray to light the city streets. She knew that the mate candidate standing just inside the door had viewed her image and had agreed to consider her as a mate…despite her looks.

She smiled wryly.

Or maybe *because* of her looks! Since he was part of the program, he might be a bit of an anomaly himself, either in his appearance or his behavior—or both. But she didn't care about any of that. She was committed to keeping her promise.

Dropping her gaze to her dark, knee-length skirt, she shook her head.

How could she have allowed them to wipe him from her memory…all those times in the past? Four times!

Hardin.

At the same time, she wondered how she could live without him.

But she'd keep her promise and keep his memory. And somehow she'd find her way back to him one day. Of that she was certain. Somehow she knew they would someday be reunited—just as she was certain she'd never stop loving him.

When she heard careful footsteps crossing the room, she roused herself to speak. "Before you decide about me, there are two things you should know." When the mate candidate didn't answer she went on. "I want to name our first child Hardin."

"I can live with that," he answered but she barely registered his words before she plunged ahead, determined to get her conditions out and in the open.

"And you should probably know…I don't believe I'll ever love you."

The man stopped moving and the room was silent for several moments.

"Any questions?" she followed up.

"I think I might be able to change your mind on that one," he finally said. "At least, I plan to spend the rest of my life trying."

Finally, she recognized his voice. Finally she was in his arms with a mouthful of questions—but they were going to have to wait because, at the moment, her mouth was full of his tongue.

Finally he broke from her, breathless, laughing. "And I do have *one* question," he taunted her, "*Miss* December."

She nodded her head quickly, her eyes latched onto his sexy, curving smile. "Yes," she laughed. "Yes, yes, yes!"

He shook his head. "Try to behave, December. You have to wait for the question before you can answer it," he lectured.

"Yes!" She laughed and shouted and squealed all at the same time.

"Okay," he finally relented with a grin. "In that case, Kansas, will you agree to be my mate?"

Miss April

ꙮ

Trademarks Acknowledgement

~

The author acknowledges the trademarked status and trademark owners of the following wordmarks mentioned in this work of fiction:

Triumph TR6: British Leyland.

Nikon: Nikon Inc.

VISA: Visa International Service Association

Chapter One

ℌ

"Do you realize," he murmured in a low deep rumble, leaning over the counter to put his face close to hers, "that our relationship has outlasted all my relationships with *all* of my other girlfriends?"

"All of your other girlfriends put together!" April corrected him with a warm laugh.

He laughed in return, a rich male sound that made her heart stutter. "That's probably true. Put together," he confirmed. "You and I have had this thing going for—"

"Two years, three months and eight days," April filled in for him, trying to keep her voice light while the rest of her was just about swooning over the carnal creature standing on the other side of the counter.

He pushed back the sleeve of his soft leather jacket and regarded his elegant watch. "And thirty-five minutes," he instructed her in a stern voice of reproof. "So, when are you going to go out with me?"

"When are you going to quit smoking?" she challenged him as she threw a pack of cigarettes onto the counter and slid the small green box in his direction.

"The moment you agree to go out with me," he answered affably.

"Mr. D. Cristofer," she announced with a lifted eyebrow, "it appears we are at an impasse."

"I don't actually smoke them, you know," he told her conspiratorially. "They're just an excuse to stop in and visit you every morning. You should see the back seat of my car."

"D'you mean to tell me," she enquired, waving the pack of cigarettes at him, "the back seat of your Triumph is littered with full packs of cigarettes?"

"Not at all. I just want you to see the back seat of my car." He leaned forward again and she was almost overwhelmed by the heat he radiated along with pure, concentrated sex appeal. "It was just *made* for a woman like you."

Swallowing hard, April squinted out the window in the direction of his vintage Triumph. "But your car is tiny!" she pointed out.

His face came that much closer to hers. So close she could smell the faint hint of peppermint on his breath. Weak-kneed, she couldn't help but imagine how that peppermint would taste on her lips. "You could bend your knees," he suggested with a warm wink and a sultry smile.

Fighting to keep her wits about her despite her very female response to his overpoweringly male presence, she shot a look through the window of the convenience store in which she worked. "I'd *have* to bend my knees if you expected me to sit in that back seat!"

"I wasn't expecting you to sit," he said in a sin-weighted whisper, "I was more imagining you on your back with your legs around my hips." He lifted his wide shoulders in a slow shrug. "But if you want to do it sitting, we could try it out."

For at least two seconds she stared at the counter, wordless as she swallowed down a hard lump of lust and her body responded to this suggestion. Her libido obviously appreciated this *particular* idea, she noted as a heavy, damp heat collected between her legs. Not that he hadn't given her plenty of ideas in the past. And that was *before* he started talking! It wasn't like she needed his help creating erotic images involving his naked body up against hers. Even when he wasn't filling her head with his own variety of illicit fantasies, her ready imagination was doing a very competent job of providing her with ideas of her own. Lots of ideas. In explicit, graphic detail.

Feigning disgust, April slapped his cigarettes down on the counter. The smack of sound was a sharp punctuation mark signifying that their exchange was over. She pushed the credit card slip toward him. "That's twenty-three, ninety for the gas, gum and cigarettes." Trying for playful, she returned his challenging smile as he signed the white slip of paper—D. Cristofer—without once looking at it.

"Have a good day, Mr. Cristofer," she told him.

Scraping his hand through brown hair that just reached the soft leather collar of his jacket, the tanned Adonis straightened to smile down on her a final time. As though he didn't already know her name, eyes the hue of sea foam lingered cheekily at her left breast where she wore her name on a rectangle of white plastic.

"You too, Miss April."

April watched him stride toward the door as she served the next customer. There ought to be a law against looking like that, she decided, drawing in a breath heavy with arousal. Men shouldn't be permitted to have eyelashes that thick *or* that curly. And why should deep, expressive eyes like those be wasted on a man? Not that they were wasted, she corrected herself quickly.

Definitely not wasted.

His blue-green eyes were deep and knowing and absolutely enthralling. But it was the man's oh-my-god mouth set firmly in his square jaw that really got her going. How could a mouth look so rugged and mean one minute and so sinfully sensual the next—when the hard edge of his curving lips hooked up into an arrogantly teasing smile?

There ought to be a law against a man looking so entirely bed-ready and oozing masculine pheromones. Eau de testosterone. The sort of heady, male-animal scent that made a woman feel like rubbing up against some naked skin in a feline attempt to mark herself so she could proclaim to the world "Don't waste your time here. I am claimed and taken". With this thought, she shook her head as she followed him out of the store with her eyes.

Through the glass front of the convenience store, she could see him open the door of his little blue coupe and drop into the driver's seat. She leaned forward to see who was occupying the passenger seat next to him this morning and nodded as she glimpsed a shining tangle of blonde hair. Strawberry blonde, she noted. And that made strawberry ripple the "flavor of the month". Last month was blackberry.

Tucking the long sweep of her straight hair behind her ears, she considered her own flavor. That would make her…orange sherbet, she decided, should she ever decide to shock Mr. D. Cristofer and take him up on his offer. Quickly making change for the next customer, she snorted loud enough to elicit a startled look from the balding man on the opposite side of the counter.

She couldn't help but wonder exactly what "Mr. Flavor of the Month" would do if she were to actually take him up on his offer. Mr. Oh-so-smooth. Mr. Never-at-a-loss-for-words—every one of which was suggestive! He'd probably swallow his peppermint gum! The idea made her smile and the customer smiled back at her before turning for the door. Grabbing up a large box of packaged pretzels, she headed across the store to refresh the snack display.

It would be interesting to see the glib Mr. D. Cristofer at a loss for words, she speculated. The man was all ease and confidence, from the top of his unruly hair to the end of those long legs that took him everywhere with a cocky sauntering stride. The guy was as smooth as smoke and just as elusive. Every morning without fail, he pulled up in front of the convenience store, strolled in as though he knew he was god's gift to women and...made her day—really. He was only there long enough to throw a package of peppermint gum on the counter and order a pack of cigarettes. But in those scant few minutes, the man gave her a reason for getting up every morning as he challenged her to keep up with a short volley of banter that covered topics ranging from the most recent current events to alternate and suggestive uses for pretzels.

And asked her when she was going to go out with him.

One of these days she was going to surprise him.

Not that she believed she'd actually ever achieve the exalted status of "flavor of the month" with a guy like that. Not at all. She'd be lucky if she made "sample of the week" and, to be honest, she'd happily settle for "taste of the day"...or night.

But one of these days she was going to surprise him. Just as soon as she worked up her nerve, she thought, shoving the colorful plastic bags onto their hangers with a little more vigor than was required. Sure, she'd like to surprise him, wipe that glib expression from his beautiful face, watch that easy smile turn into stunned shock—uncertainty.

There was only one thing stopping her, she thought, staring at her name pin stuck onto the maroon company shirt she wore. Fear. The fear that his shock and uncertainty would turn into horrified realization. Denial. A quick explanation of a date he'd just remembered. A hurried apology followed by the sound of burning rubber as he peeled out of the parking lot, leaving nothing behind but two dark, smoking lines burned into the gray asphalt.

It wasn't like she was the most beautiful woman in the world. She'd seen the sort of women who occupied the passenger seat of that little blue Triumph. *They* were the most beautiful women in the world. Nevertheless, she intended to take him up on his offer—one day. One day about a year from now, when she'd lost about twenty-five pounds. Until then, she wouldn't risk ruining what they had. She wouldn't risk the chance that he'd walk out that door and never come back...and she'd never again have even this very small thing she shared with Mr. D. Cristofer.

Chapter Two

ꙮ

Two days later, April was watching for him as he pulled up in his TR6. After having missed work the day before, she was more than a little anxious to get him in her sights and was relieved when he showed up right on schedule. From her station behind the counter, she could see the light frown marring his handsome features as he tilted his head, peering into the storefront as he made his way along the sidewalk that led to the glass doors. When his eyes connected with hers, his lips curled into a smile but it did little to dissipate the troubled expression that still lingered on his face.

His tense, hurried stride slowed to a saunter as he entered the store. Grabbing a narrow package of gum, he headed for the counter. "Where were you yesterday?" he asked her in a strangely casual tone that sounded forced as well as false.

She grinned and winked. "Slept in."

"Until two o'clock?" He was still smiling and it still didn't look very convincing.

"You were here at two o'clock?" she asked with surprise.

He nodded. "I dropped by in the afternoon just to…nobody had heard from you all day. That's a lot of time to spend in bed," he pointed out, still trying to laugh and still sounding worried as well as a bit miffed.

"And it was worth *every* minute of it," she drawled suggestively, hoping to make him laugh.

But he wasn't laughing. His mouth flattened as he stared at her.

Reaching over her head for a pack of cigarettes, she started scanning in his order.

"I won't be needing those," he told her. "I don't smoke. I never did."

Confused, her wrist hovered uncertainly above the barcode reader as she searched his face.

"I only came in here to see you," he told her as he dug into his pocket and threw a dollar bill on the counter then turned away with a concrete air of finality.

With her mouth open, April stared at his broad back then swiftly made his change and slipped around the counter as quickly as she could. "Hey," she shouted as she pushed through the store's doors and onto the sidewalk outside.

Standing in the parking lot, he paused, his fingers locked around the door handle of his automobile.

"Hey. You…forgot your change." She held her hand out to him but his own hands remained at his sides as his serious gaze swept her face accusingly.

"Who were you sleeping with?" he asked. "And why?"

"Wh-why?"

"Yes. Why. Why were you sleeping with someone else…instead of me?"

April stared at his face. As far as she could tell, he was serious. Dead serious.

"I had a flat tire," she said faintly. "I had a flat tire and never made it into work. I wasn't…in bed. I wasn't sleeping in."

His jaw shifted gears a few times as he worked his gum between his teeth, staring at the handle of his car then glancing up at her to check her face. His stormy gaze was shielded and his expression was wary as he considered her with brooding eyes the color of wind-tossed seas.

"I was kidding," she told him.

He nodded, opened his car door and reached inside. With a ballpoint pen in his grip, he pulled her hand into his and took the coins wrapped in her fist. Then, keeping her hand, he wrote ten numbers on the heel of her palm. "This is my cell number. Next time you get a flat tire," he stated, "you call me." Finally, the corners of his rugged mouth turned up into a smile. "Okay?"

Dumbly, she nodded.

"See you tomorrow, Miss April," he said, opening the car door and settling into the black leather seat. "And when are you going to go out with me?" he asked, shooting her a sexy grin that would have made a satyr proud.

"How about tonight?" she muttered to herself as the door slammed and he rolled down his window.

"What was that?"

"How about tonight?" she voiced more strongly.

Her stomach dropped as she watched his eyes widen, his face go blank and his smile drop right off the scale. "I…I have plans for tonight," he murmured, his voice as well as his eyes filled with horror. "Jesus. I—"

Nodding quickly, she backed away from the car and turned.

"April," he shouted as she hurried toward the store. His car door slammed again then his hand was on her arm, turning her before she could escape into the store. "I'll change them," he said, talking quickly. "I'll change my plans. Give me your address. I'll pick you up at six."

Forcing herself to respond calmly, she related her address in an unwavering voice as he smiled at her without writing it down. He was grinning as he backed away from her. "Pick you up at six," he told her again. "Wear…black. Something long and sexy and…black. I'll buy you dinner."

* * * * *

Long and sexy and black, April sang to herself. *Pick you up at six. Pick you up at six.*

It was hard not to be excited. Long and sexy and black meant somewhere elegant and romantic and expensive for dinner! She was going somewhere elegant and romantic and expensive with absolutely the most drop-dead gorgeous man on the face of the earth! She could hardly wait for her shift to end at three o'clock so she could get home and start preparing herself for her date.

Not that she expected much more than dinner. She wasn't going to allow herself to be unrealistic about the whole situation. It was probably going to be one of those one-night-things. But she was determined to enjoy every minute of her one-night-thing and make it last a full twelve hours followed by a drive home in the morning…and not one minute earlier!

She even had the dress! Okay. It was older. But it was a great dress! It had always been a great dress with sharp, clean lines that did a very adequate job of concealing her thunder thighs along with a boat neckline that cut across the top of her shoulders and balanced her substantial breasts. And for sex appeal, it had a scoop in the back that plunged all the way down to the two dimples tucked below her waist.

She was still trying to decide what to do with her hair when the doorbell rang. She stared at the door to her apartment. It was five-thirty.

Cautiously, she crept to the door, turned the handle and cracked the door open an inch to peek outside. Mr. D. Cristofer stood with his back to her, his hands buried in the side pockets of his khaki slacks, the jacket of his dark blazer flaring out over the strong wrists he had shoved into his pockets. Slowly, he turned and smiled.

"You're early," she squeaked.

"I'm sorry," he apologized, the long line of his mouth curving up into a lazy smile. "My timing's usually better. But I assure you it won't happen again. At least it won't happen again tonight."

Opening the door, she wrinkled her nose at him. "I was going to ask you to come in," she teased, "but considering the mood you're in, it might be safer just to ask you to enter."

He smirked as he strode through the door. "Come. Enter. Either works for me," he said slyly. Stopping just inside the door, he sighed contentedly as he considered her small living room.

"Take a chair," she told him. "Make yourself comfortable."

"I'd be more comfortable if I took a seat," he drawled, raising his eyebrows and letting his sea foam eyes drift playfully to the round curves of her bottom. "Do you have any to spare?"

"If you were more observant," she slung back at him, "you'd have noticed I have *more* than enough to spare. I'm surprised you missed that little fact."

"Sweetheart. There's nothing little about your…"

She spun to face him, threatening him with a lifted eyebrow. He let his gaze drop to her chest. "Facts," he finally finished.

She made a face. "Is that the best you could come up with?"

"Oh no. No." He shook his head and a few strands of brown hair spilled onto his forehead. "I could come up with a whole lot more. Just let me know when you're ready, and I promise I'll be up for it."

"Up for it, my ass," she grumbled as she turned again.

"You offering, then?" His voice followed her down the hall.

She ignored him. "Do I need a coat?" she called back to him.

"Absolutely," he advised. "A coat is an absolute requirement."

"Is it chilly outside, then?"

"Not at all. But it will be nice helping you into your coat. And when you get outside and realize how warm it is, it will be nice helping you out of it again."

In her bedroom, April smiled at her happy reflection caught in the round mirror over her dressing table. Pulling her long fall of red hair in front of her shoulder, she opened her closet door.

"One thing leads to another," he continued in a deep drawl that wound its way down the hall into her bedroom. "And once I've taken your coat off, who knows where it might lead?"

Deciding her hair could just swing loose, she came back up the hall with a jacket over her arm. "Mr. D. Cristofer," she scolded, "*you* have a one-track mind."

"I won't deny it," he retorted, opening the door to her apartment and ushering her outside. "And if you think my one-track mind is impressive, wait until you see what I can do with my hands."

With those words, he settled his large warm hand in the small of her back as though it belonged there as he guided her toward his car, waiting in the parking lot. With his warm touch on the tingling skin at the base of her spine, along with his teasing, flirty banter, April felt like a bottle of frothy champagne. Ready to go off. Bubbly with excitement and laughter.

This was going to be the perfect night.

* * * * *

Twenty minutes later April was chewing on her bottom lip. Uncertainly, she peered through the car's passenger side window at the elegant brick home as her date made his way around the back of the car to her door. Built in the twenties or thirties, the gray brick house stood twenty feet off the street. A stone walk cut through a deep lawn up to the steps of a sheltered veranda.

"Where are we?" she asked when he opened her door.

"My place," he told her lightly. Taking her hand, he pulled her out onto the sidewalk.

"But, I thought—I mean…I assumed we'd be having dinner."

He nodded as he turned. "There's a place around the corner that makes great Chinese *and*…they deliver."

"Oh," she said faintly as every single frothy bubble of laughter and excitement imploded inside her, leaving her with a breathlessly flat feeling of disappointment. "Oh." Her stomach clenched as she came to an unsettling conclusion.

He didn't want to be seen with her.

He didn't want to take her out to dinner in a public restaurant—let alone somewhere elegant, romantic *or* expensive. All at once, her mood fell along with the smile she'd been wearing since he'd walked into her apartment. She couldn't help but feel a wee bit betrayed. Why had he suggested the formal wear? All at once she felt incredibly uncomfortable. All at once she felt like a complete idiot—dressed in a long, floor-length gown to eat takeout in his living room.

Moving ahead of her to his veranda, he climbed the steps and keyed the door open then ushered her inside, following to flip some light switches into the on position. Immediately, before she could even take in the interior of his home, he was against her, pressing his body into hers, his hands on her waist, his breath in her hair.

The man was up for it all right, just as he'd promised in her apartment. She could feel the tall, thick ridge of his penis hard against her belly as he pressed her into the door's unyielding surface. The man was up for a discreetly private fuck behind the closed doors of his home—the *barely closed* doors of his home.

Giving up his hold on her waist, he leaned his upper body away from her long enough to get his hands on either side of her face. His eyes were downcast as he tilted his head slightly and studied her mouth with what appeared to be avaricious interest.

"I…thought we'd be going to dinner," she interrupted in a small brave voice.

"I only said I'd *buy* you dinner," he rasped in little more than a whisper. "The Chinese food is on its way. I don't want to share you," he explained as his chest crushed against hers. "I've waited too long for the chance to get together with you and I'm not going to waste it in a public place."

As he moved his lips toward hers, she shook her head. More like he didn't want to be seen with her in a public place, she thought blankly. "I…I think I'd like to leave now," she told him solemnly, turning her face just before his mouth reached hers.

His face fell in utter shock. She almost felt sorry for him. Bet that doesn't happen often, she told herself. Then he looked a little panicked, from which fact she concluded that he didn't have any other options for the night. Evidently he didn't have another quick fuck lined up—someone to replace her in his bed.

"I'd like to leave," she repeated while he was still staring at her, open-mouthed and apparently stunned.

"Wh-why? April. What did I say?"

When she turned within the cage of his arms and reached for the doorknob, he was right there behind her, reaching over her head, planting a hand in the middle of the door and putting his weight against it. The next thing she felt were his lips in her hair, close to her ear.

"What's wrong?" he murmured, his peppermint breath damp and erotically soft against her temple. She stared at the door's smooth, polished surface as he crowded her against it.

"I didn't think it was just going to be…just going to be…"

"You and me?" he suggested with a warm laugh. "Did you want me to invite some of my friends?"

Inside the cage of his arms she struggled but he only pushed against her more tightly, his imposing erection finding a warm, comfortable place between the cheeks of her bottom, taking up permanent residence between the globes of her ass.

"I'm teasing," he insisted as she wiggled beneath him. "And if you don't stop wiggling, you're going to start something that *I* can't stop."

After a bit of a struggle, she managed to get herself turned around and facing him again.

"I assumed you had an ulterior motive in asking me out," she admitted valiantly.

"Did you?" he murmured, dragging the rough-smooth surface of his lips down her cheek, putting his warm breath on her neck. "Clever girl."

"But I thought there'd be, there might be…more."

"But there is," he insisted in a sexy growl as he pulled his open mouth down her neck, teasing her skin with his warm, heated breath. "There's a whole lot more," he told her, flexing his knees and pushing the hard bulge of his cock into her rise.

"I didn't think it was going to be *just* sex," she finally blurted out.

There was an instant's stunned silence.

"You have *got* to be kidding," he panted roughly, his breath moist on her collarbone. "Tell me you're kidding, April. I thought that was clear. I thought we'd both made that clear. I thought we'd been talking about this for two years, three months and…and ten days. April, I— "

Abruptly he stopped, straightening his legs as he ran his knuckle along her cheekbone, then stopping to stare at the moisture shining on his wet finger. "What's this?" he asked wonderingly. His eyes searched her face and widened as his gaze followed the path of a second runaway tear. Finally his face was serious. "What's wrong?" he asked without a trace of humor.

"Nothing," she told him, staring down to avoid looking at his face and finding herself gazing at the bulging line of his fly. "It's just obvious that you…don't want to be seen with me…in public."

"Don't want to— " For several moments he was silent as she stared doggedly downward. She felt him nod a few times. "It's not so much I don't want to be seen with you," he finally admitted, "in public…so much as I don't think I could keep my hands off you—in public. But if you want to give it a go, I'm willing to try. I…can't promise I'll behave myself. If worse comes to worse, I can always put you in my lap and we can pretend we're having a conversation while we're…not. But I know a nice place," he said, suddenly brusque.

"It's too late now," she told him, staring miserably at the dark floor. "You'll never get a reservation this late on a Friday night. "And…and…you've already ordered Chinese."

"I know a place where we can get in," he told her. "And I'll leave a couple of twenties taped to the front door in an envelope. How do you feel about cold Chinese for breakfast?” he asked her with a brief, tentative smile. When she didn’t answer, he strafed her with his searing gaze before he stepped away. “I’ll get that envelope,” he told her then walked away, reaching up to drag both hands through his hair.

Chapter Three

ꙮ

She should have insisted that he take her home, April decided an hour later when they were sitting at a window table in Maxime's. You couldn't get much more elegant and romantic and expensive than Maxime's Downtown! Guiding her into the crowded foyer, her date had caught the headwaiter's eye. Immediately, the immaculately attired young man had made his way over to greet them. "Mr. Cristofer," he said with a wink, "table for two?" And with this greeting, the young man led them past half a dozen patrons waiting to be seated. Following the headwaiter's crisp white jacket, April's date steered her with a hand around her waist.

The view from Maxime's huge floor-to-ceiling windows might have been breathtaking if April wasn't feeling so self-conscious. The small city's modest towers cut black geometric shapes out of the swirling orange and purples in the western sky. After pushing her chair underneath her, her date had stood a moment gazing at the sunset, his eyes reflecting orange in their blue-green depths. Following his gaze, she looked into the western sky. "You can almost see Phippsburg from here," she offered awkwardly. "My mother lives out there."

He gave her a silent nod before he took his seat.

He'd been quiet on the drive over.

He was quiet after they ordered, fingering the stem of his wine glass as he stared at it, a sulky scowl edging his hard features. It was the sort of expression a man gets when he feels he's been cheated. When he feels he's been cheated out of *sex* and is wondering what the hell he's doing, sitting in an expensive restaurant wasting his time *and* his money.

When he turned his wrist to check the time, April wanted to die, then and there. Turning nervously in her seat to review escape options, she considered excusing herself to visit the ladies room then making a dash for the front door. It was a bit early in the evening, but there might be a taxi parked at the curb.

"Don't even think about it," he growled when she cast a second glance over her shoulder at the restaurant's exit. "Don't even think about sneaking out of here without explaining to me *why* you think I wouldn't want to be seen with you."

"I'm s-sorry," she stammered.

His eyes were still downcast, his expression still discontent—both hard and hurt. "You ought to be sorry," he grumbled to the lace tablecloth. "How blunt can you get? It's obvious *to me* that you think *I'm* shallow. Thanks for that," he said snidely, snagging her with moody eyes as he tipped some wine into his mouth.

She could only stare at that handsome, sulking mouth while he pulled in his cheeks and savored the wine an instant before swallowing. Apparently waiting for a response, he eyed her darkly.

"You…you could have any woman you want," she mumbled, as though that was an excuse, or at least an explanation for her behavior.

For an instant his eyes narrowed on her. "Do you really think so?" he drawled in an unkind voice. He leaned back in his chair with a long, lazy, condescending smile. "Any woman? Any woman at all? In that case…do you think I could have a strong, exciting, opinionated, interesting woman? A bright, witty, well-informed woman? A woman who makes me laugh and—as long as I'm asking for *any* woman—could she share my point of view on most matters without hesitating to disagree with me when her opinion differed?" When she didn't answer, his smile took on a nasty edge. "And could I have all of that along with great curves?" He paused for her reaction. "In that case, I think I'd be happy.

"I'm a bit juvenile when it comes to curves," he confessed dispassionately. "I've dated some great-looking women, the kind of women who turn heads, but there's nothing on earth like getting your hands around a woman with curves." With those words, his gaze lingered on her chest.

"Well, if you like large breasts," she told him with a courageous smile, "you've come to the right place."

He nodded. "It's not just the…breasts," he answered with more than a trace of male arrogance. "I like the whole package. I like to get my hands full of a woman, front and back. I like a great ass as well as huge tits." Now he focused on her mouth. "And I love full lips.

"Of course, if I could have any woman, she'd have to like sex," he mentioned philosophically, shifting in his seat. "Ideally, she wouldn't be afraid to make love with the lights on," he said in a low slice of quiet, "and wouldn't close her eyes when I'm on her—inside her. And, as long as I'm asking, I wouldn't mind a woman who likes to suck cock. Not just a woman who's willing, but a woman who likes it. Know anyone like that?"

She stared at him breathlessly, not daring to tip her head in either direction. Not brave enough to indicate her answer with either a positive or negative tilt of her chin.

Abruptly, a hand appeared before her face and she almost jumped as the waiter placed a huge plate under her nose. She blinked down at the tiny offering of Coquilles St. Jacques in the middle of the large porcelain circle.

"I have nothing to prove," he continued quietly. "I don't have to show other men, or other women for that matter, that I can get a beautiful date. That's a given. I can go out with whomever I like." He paused and gave her an accusatory glare. "Which is what I'm doing tonight."

"I'm sorry," she said again, feeling like a prize idiot. Feeling like a prize idiot with no appetite whatsoever. Biting at her bottom lip, she stared down at the beautiful display of elegant food while she picked up a fork and used it to prod at the fat scallops swimming in a fragrant white sauce. It was funny, but she couldn't remember Coquilles St. Jacques ever looking quite so blurry before.

She heard a very distinctly male rumble from the other side of the table. "God, that's sexy," he was saying in a voice both rough and warm. Blinking back a wash of tears, she chanced a quick glance at him and found him no longer leaning back in his chair. Instead, his elbow was propped on the table as he ignored his own appetizer and stared hungrily at her mouth. Quickly, she jabbed at a scallop and stuffed it between her lips. In return, he gave her a low growl of laughter. The rough-edged male sound was the epitome of sex incarnate. That rumble started a tremor of sensation at the bottom of her spine that wrapped around her hips in a very loving and very passionate embrace. In short, she felt like she was melting from the waist down.

"What about you?" he asked her, playing with his smoked salmon for several seconds before finally putting a tiny orange fragment on the end of his fork and lifting it to his perfectly masculine mouth. "What kind of man would you choose if you could have any man you want?"

Chewing carefully, she didn't answer.

"Would he be anything like me?"

She nodded at the table. "He'd be a lot like you," she admitted.

"Tell me about him," he commanded, returning his fork to the lace tablecloth.

"Oh…" she started tentatively. "He'd…be tall with brown hair and strong opinions. He'd be clever and funny and witty. He'd be unpredictable and surprise me at every turn. He'd pay me a ridiculous amount of attention as well as far more compliments than I deserve.

"At the same time, he'd be sensitive and maybe even a little vulnerable. He'd have a rough edge…a bit of a temper. Not much. Just enough to make him interesting."

"Is that all?"

She shook her head as she finally lifted her gaze to his. "He'd be good in bed," she told him.

For several long thick seconds they stared at each other. "I'm really not very hungry," she finally confessed in a very small, helpless voice.

"Oh Jesus," he said, staring at her like he could eat her alive. Carefully he pushed back his chair and pulled her to her feet. Falling back into his own chair, he dragged her down into his lap. "I knew this would happen," he grumbled against her neck. "I tried to warn you."

When he pulled her into his lap, she found herself facing into the restaurant, her back to the huge windows. His right arm was next to the window but his right hand was in his lap, under her bottom, pressed tight against her pussy. When he shifted his legs apart beneath his hand, she lost her balance for a brief instant and, reacting instinctively, her hands moved to clutch onto the nearest available surface. While her right hand locked on the table, she found her left hand wrapped around what felt like a solid, steel-hard bar. Realizing she had a hold of his cock, her cheeks warmed as she felt herself blush. He was as hard as a cast iron poker.

A small choking sound was on his lips as his head tipped forward slightly and he blinked several times. "No," he told her when she loosened her grip on him. "Don't you dare. Don't you dare let go," he whispered roughly. "It feels too goddamn good. You're the one who insisted on a public place. Now you can just deal with it."

"We should leave," she murmured breathlessly, hanging her head, the side of her face touching his forehead.

"Yeah, we should. But I'm not walking across Maxime's with this huge fucking hard-on. And I'll tell you something else, April. Even if we were to leave now, there's no way I'd make it all the way home. Not like this."

"Why are you so hard?" she complained, tightening her grip on him while he sucked in a breath.

"Why are you so sexy?" he countered with obvious difficulty.

"Me? I didn't do anything. This isn't my fault."

"No? You don't think so? Well let me tell you, sweetheart. Something's got me hard as a rock and I don't think it's the headwaiter."

With those words, he adjusted his right hand in the space he'd created between his spread legs and cupped her pussy in his long fingers. Reaching across the table with his left hand, he speared one of her scallops on the end of a fork and fed it to her. She felt a thin line of warm sauce start down over the edge of her lip and reached for it with her tongue, only to meet his, lapping at her lower lip. Slowly, he polished off her bottom lip with the full press of his flattened tongue and used its tip to push hers back into her mouth. Then the hard edge of his teeth caught her lip in a gentle clamp, tugging at her flesh, dragging the bottom of her lip between his teeth for an instant before he let her free again. Beneath her, his hand was still working her over, moving, holding, petting, massaging the thick lips of her sex, his fingers shifting and coaxing as he played with her full, sensitive flesh.

"Do you like that?" he asked her, feeding her another scallop and laughing in a low, musical rasp when she closed her eyes and moaned. "I'll take that as a yes," he muttered with a voice both breathless and strained. "You're getting hot," he informed her in a murmur, "and damp. I can feel you right through the heavy fabric of your dress." He put his lips against her ear. "Are you going to come? Are you going to come right here in the restaurant? Let me know because if you are, I want to come with you."

With these words, he popped the final scallop in her mouth then reached down with his left hand to reposition her grip on his shaft. "Right there," he told her in an abrasive whisper. "Just give me a stroke or two and I'm with you."

His fingers dug in deeper, moved faster, concentrating on the top of her pussy where her fat, sodden lips slid over her clitoris. "Come on, April," he told her. "Don't hold back. Don't *make* me fuck you. Don't make me unzip that dress and pull my dick out in the middle of the restaurant."

"Oh no," she whispered as she accelerated toward climax, turning her face to hide it against the damp skin of his temple. His head turned and his lips found hers, covering her mouth as he rushed her forward. Her hand tightened around his erection as she started to come in jolting spasms, jerking a bit and pulling on his long, tightly cased flesh.

She felt him stiffen as he put a low groan into her mouth and his garbled words of lust were stifled, bottled up inside his throat as his cock expanded beneath her hand then pulsed hotly several times.

Seconds later they were panting together, temple to damp forehead, pasted together as they fought for breath. "I can't believe we just did that," he groaned, angling his head and dragging his lips to rest moistly beneath her ear. "You bring out the worst in me, woman."

"B-bring out the worst in you?"

"Yeah. And now it's all over the inside of my pants. Jesus," he complained. "We'd better get out of here before someone asks us to leave."

Lifting her head carefully, April peeked across the restaurant from behind the curtain of her spilled hair. But the nearby diners continued their murmured conversation as though they hadn't noticed the two lovers going after each other, hot and heavy.

Then she was sliding off his lap as he stood suddenly and headed through the restaurant, towing her by the wrist and only slowing when he dragged her past the headwaiter's station. "You have my VISA number," he threw over his shoulder to the smiling young man. "Thank you, James. Don't forget the tip." With these words of instruction, he pushed April through the front doors, his hand spread over half of her bottom.

Chapter Four

ꟗ

"You were right about my ulterior motives," April's date told her as he grabbed the large brown bag that had been left on the doorstep and ushered her into his home for the second time that evening. He placed the paper bag on a low, marble-topped cabinet just inside the door. The rumpled sack emitted a pleasant mixture of faint aromas—fried egg rolls, sesame and shrimp.

They stood inside the large foyer. A staircase descended from the floor above, a black wrought iron balustrade gracing its sweeping curve. As she waited for her date to hang up her jacket, April moved to better view a few pieces of colorful art hanging on one of the entry's muted gray walls. Impossible to ignore on the severe gray foil, the bright oil pastels called to her as she moved toward them. Her pumps clicked on the polished floor, tiled with large slabs of charcoal marble which was threaded with silvery veins of white quartz.

"Exactly how wealthy are you?" she exclaimed.

He followed her gaze to three pastels on the wall.

"These are…Dalton's work. Aren't they?"

"Do you like them?"

She nodded as she pulled her eyes back to him. "I like…what he does with orange," she told him. "Does that make any sense?"

He only frowned at her as he tilted his head appraisingly. "I think I know what you mean," he finally told her. With a hand in the small of her back, he guided her into the living room that opened out of the foyer. "But getting back to my ulterior motives," he started, "your dress had a lot to do with my motives for tonight."

"I wondered why you suggested formal wear," she told him. He left her in the middle of the room as he moved to a large heavy credenza and opened the doors to pull out two crystal wine glasses. While she surveyed his comfortable living room, he poured out two glasses of rich, dark merlot.

The room was long and well lit with built-in bookcases faced with glass doors, the wood a deep cherry color and polished to a high gloss, the plain, simple handles fashioned from hammered copper. Underfoot, her heels wobbled in the deep, luxurious nap of the pale gray carpet. Before the wide windows sat a long, curving sofa of soft leather the color of cream, as well as a wide-armed chair to match. A few pieces of heavy antique furniture took their regal place along the walls, and in the corner an expensive digital camera sat on a tripod. Wobbling over in that direction, April peered at two more Daltons on the wall behind the camera.

Pulling in a deep breath, she held it in her lungs, savoring the flavor of his home. Light peppermint along with something deeper, richer—hidden in the background. Something satisfyingly earthy, a scent that she couldn't quite identify.

Joining her, he put a sparkling goblet in her hand and asked her, "What color panties are you wearing?"

"I beg your pardon?" she returned with a blink.

"What color panties are you wearing?" he repeated with a comfortable smile. "I want to know more about you. Believe it or not, you can learn a lot about a woman by checking out her underwear drawer. You can tell even more by what she's wearing under her clothing. Take that black evening gown you're wearing, for instance. Most women would wear black panties. Conservative. Predictable. But it could be worse. The woman who would wear white panties with a dress like that would be hopelessly practical, unimaginative."

"What if she didn't have anything else?"

"That would be particularly tragic," he sighed with false pathos and a twinkle gleaming in his blue-green gaze.

"And what would it mean if a woman wore no panties at all with a dress like this?"

"*Don't* get me excited," he admonished her sternly.

She laughed. "What would it mean?" she insisted, sipping at the mellow old red.

"It would mean the woman was an optimist by nature with a *lot* of self-confidence. It would mean the lady planned to get laid." The long line of his mouth kicked up into a slow smile. "So tell me, am I that lucky? And are you that confident?"

Again she laughed. "Not quite that confident. My panties are green," she confessed.

"Green!" His eyes misted as he seemed to travel a great distance from his body. "Green," he murmured. "Green on black. That's an interesting combination. Then you didn't choose them for the color," he told her as his gaze hugged her hips. "I'm guessing you chose them for the fit. That dress is…tight to say the least. Perfectly, deliciously tight."

"You're amazing," she told him with a grin. "And you're…half right."

"Half right?"

"I had a pair of red panties that would have worked but—"

"Red is for stop and green is for go."

"Right again." She hesitated before she made the next confession. "I didn't want to broadcast any negative signals," she explained with a shy smile. "No matter how subtle."

"That was very thoughtful of you," he told her almost as if he hadn't heard her. "Green," he whispered lovingly, staring at her hips with dreamy, unfocused eyes. "Show me," he demanded suddenly.

"Wh-at?"

"Show me," he told her brusquely.

"What do you mean? Show you?"

"I don't know, exactly. Show me in whatever manner you wish."

She started a little laugh but cut it off short when he took the wine glass out of her hand and placed it on a low table in front of the sofa.

"Get comfortable," he advised her and she looked around at the room a little self-consciously before she finally chose to place herself beside the credenza, leaning against it as she rucked the stiff, dark poplin up her legs, chewing on the thick pad of her bottom lip as she did so.

"No," he corrected her immediately. "Use the chair. Otherwise...you'll be uncomfortable," he explained awkwardly.

"Okay," she answered uncertainly, letting her dress fall again and moving toward the chair. For a few seconds she frowned at the chair hesitantly. Then made a decision. Turning her back to him as he waited on the other side of the room, she put a knee on the seat of the overstuffed chair. Reaching behind her with both hands, she found the top of her zipper and eased it downward, knowing she didn't have far to go before she'd be into the green zone.

"How's that?" she asked him.

"A little bit farther," he answered.

She laughed a bit and eased her zipper down another inch. "You must be able to see them by now!" she exclaimed in a low voice.

"Not quite," he told her quietly, as though he was holding his breath.

Worrying her bottom lip apprehensively, she turned her head and cast her eyes over her shoulder as she checked out her derriere.

She heard him sigh. "Perfect," he told her as he took his hands out of his pockets and moved toward her. "Perfect," he repeated when he reached her and turned her to face him. "Just absolutely fucking perfect," he said as his fingers spread to case her chin and his eyes focused on her mouth. Then he brought his mouth across hers for their first real kiss.

Considering the fact that they'd been working their way up to this point all evening, she couldn't understand why her body reacted so forcibly to his touch as well as his taste. Together they jolted at that first tentative contact as his lips barely touched hers. Then he sucked in a breath before he tilted his head and returned his lips to her mouth again. The smooth pads of his hard, sensuous lips explored hers lightly at first, as though savoring each tiny brush and stroke and nibble, as though testing and tasting, feeding his searing breath against her lips, taking her own breaths deep into his lungs. Playing with her mouth as though the kiss didn't matter, so much as the barely maintained connection, the feathered touch of his lips exploiting hers for every tactile sensation he could pull out of the experience.

Abruptly, his approach changed, as though he'd gotten as much as he needed or perhaps as much as he could take. Quite without warning, he attacked her with his kiss, mercilessly twisting his mouth on hers as his lips worked her over.

When she pulled away from him, fighting for a lungful of air, she felt his harsh humid breath on her wet lips before he slipped his hand under her shoulder and used his spread fingers to secure the back of her skull. With a growl of discontent and warning, he clamped her head so he could continue the kiss without her meddling interference, without her inconvenient attempts to get a breath into her lungs. His lips slashed across hers this time, his teeth scraping the wide bow of her upper lip as he brutally forced his way into her mouth, using his tongue to breech the moist opening and get inside her to battle with her tongue.

The rough sweep of his tongue was hot and demanding, bold and rapacious as it slid between her teeth, taking and claiming the inside of her mouth. As he rubbed his mouth against hers, she turned to putty in his hands, unconsciously melting against him, curving into his embrace, molding her body against his, giving in and giving permission for whatever would follow—consenting to his actions and inviting him to take them as far as he dared.

There was a faint tremor on his lips as a groan rumbled up from his chest and he fed the needy turbulent sound into her mouth. Then his hands were behind her, beneath the wide straps of her dress, easing them over her shoulders and down her arms. He broke the kiss again, panting roughly as he rested his forehead on the crown of her head and watched the black fabric slide down her arms, exposing the upper swell of her breasts.

As her gown slid lower, revealing the upper half of her peach-tinged areolas, he choked down a strangled sound of intensely male appreciation. He had to angle his upper body away from her to allow the dress to slide lower, exposing the whole of her large, glowing nipples to his view. Forcing his lower body to separate from hers with what appeared to be a monumental effort, he helped her gown farther down her body, tucking his hands inside her dress and urging it down over her hips. April shivered as the fabric dropped to her feet in stiff folds and she stood before him, dressed only in her green satin bikinis.

Then his hands were all over her panties as he stooped for her breast. She watched his dark head bend over her breasts and felt his warm breath wash over her areola just before he used his lips to pluck the puffy nipple into a sharp peak. At the same time, his hands smoothed over the green satin on her hips, then slid behind her to grasp her cheeks and tug them apart as his fingertips encroached into the space he'd created between the full globes of her bottom. His hands moved lower, sliding over the crimp of her ass and moving tantalizingly close to her sex. Several times he repeated the action, each time moving his fingers closer to the heat of her opening. The sensitive flesh surrounding her sex was aching with anticipation, eager for the rough stroke of his fingers over the slick fabric that shielded her entrance. Instinctively her back arched as she shuddered, feeding her full breasts against the brawny silk of his jaw at the same time her bottom curved outward—reaching for his hand, for his greedy, strafing touch.

She felt his lust-roughened laugh at her breast as he covered a full, round areola with his mouth and sucked her in deeply. His tongue and teeth rasped against her delicate skin and her back arched farther, offering him more of her bottom as he tugged her cheeks wider, stretching the opening of her vagina with a heavenly tightness as his fingers slid deeper, wonderfully close to her damp entrance.

When his fingers brushed lightly across the wet satin that covered her opening, she gasped as her body bucked once. Again he laughed as he ran the flat of his tongue over the bruised color of her ravaged nipple. "Oh god. You are *so* hot," he rasped against her skin and she couldn't help but feel a small, warm glow of pride as she gazed down on his head.

Abruptly, he pulled away, shrugging his blazer off his shoulders. Throwing his coat on the long sofa, he rolled his white sleeves up past his elbows as his gaze licked up her body like a line of fire. When he put his hands on her again, he turned her. "Put your hands on the chair's arms," he whispered against her ear. When she leaned over to comply, he followed her, bending over her and cupping his hands beneath the full, heavy weight of her breasts, playing his fingertips over her fat, hard nipples, exploring every full inch of her breasts with his palms, measuring her plump weight in his hold. Her bottom was now fitted into his groin and he rocked against her with an evocative male rhythm that twisted through her blood and wrenched at her hungry sex. The slide and drag of his hips was rough and insistent at the same time he worshiped her full breasts with the grasp and clutch of his hands.

After a few more thrusts of his hips, his rocking became more aggressive, more urgent and his hands groped at her breasts a little more roughly before he finally let them bounce free. Straightening, he gripped her hips tightly as he ground his erection against her cushioned crease, using his foot inside hers to urge her legs apart, then using his hands to stretch her cheeks again. The friction of his delicious width moving against the cushioned seam of her sex made her sigh with pleasure and whimper with need, as everything inside her settled heavily in her vagina, smoldering and begging for the burning entry of male flesh, aching to be shafted by steel and silk. Again she whimpered as her body cried out for the male at her back, the man planted firmly between her cheeks, teasing and taunting her with the promise of a dark masculine spike of pleasure only he could deliver.

Dropping her forearms into the chair, she pushed back at him, catching more of his covered shaft deeper inside her parted pussy. In answer, his hard fingers bit into the globes of her ass as he clutched her bottom and spread her wider, fitting his cloth-covered ridge into her satin-lined crease and riding into her with an undisguised male lust both animal and feral. Without meaning to, she found herself moaning and stretching, pushing back on him each time he pressed forward.

A sudden snarl of sound preceded the plunge of his hands inside her panties, as he peeled the slick satin down over her ass. Brusquely, the thick pad of his fingertip slid through the line of her sex as though testing her. It moved easily through her slippery folds. She was wet and she knew it, swimming in wet heat as his finger slipped through her slick pussy. A light burr announced his fly opening and a wisp of moaning anticipation escaped her lips as she waited, panting, silently begging for his cock. Then she felt the thick, warm press of him as he notched into her, his cock head impossibly huge as he stretched her vulva with his first wide inch. Slowly, he worked his way inside her channel in thick, straining inches as her vagina clenched and tightened and fought his entry. She groaned. It had been a while.

"Fuck," he complained worshipfully as he gave a final thrust of his hips and she felt him bang up deep inside—all the way in, drumming against her cervix. "You're so…tight." He tried to spread her legs wider but her panties held her thighs together.

Rip the panties, she instructed him silently. *Just rip the damn things off.*

Giving up on widening her stance, he pulled her cheeks again as he retracted his cock a few inches then hammered home again. He gasped, a sound of pure male pleasure, as he repeated the same pummel and thrust a few more times. As she pressed her forehead against the cool leather seat of the chair, his thumbs were between her cheeks, just above and to either side of his rampaging cock as he used them to pull her apart. She wondered if his eyes were closed or if he was watching the thick root of his shaft as he fed it into her tightly stretched vulva. Finally chancing a look over her shoulder, she caught him in the act, his eyes burning and focused on his cock as he shoved into her. And he caught her watching.

"This isn't working," he told her as he withdrew his long length and cradled his wet shaft in his hand. "Let's get rid of those panties." Pulling her up by the hips, he worked her panties down her legs then fitted himself against her as they stood together, his front to her back. His cock was damp and steamy where it reached into the small of her back and his hands were between their bodies, stroking her rounded bottom longingly.

Turning her with his hands on her waist, he guided her down to sit in the chair, then dropped to his knees, leaning forward and mouthing a nipple with restless bursts of breath and the abrasive drag of his tongue. At the same time, he caught her behind one knee and eased it carefully up onto the arm's fat upholstered arm. "Don't fight me," he warned her when she stiffened. "Don't fight me," he repeated, running his fingers down the taut stretched muscle of her inner thigh. Then his hand was behind her other knee, urging it gently up onto the chair's other arm.

There was a deep, dull pounding in her chest and she shifted her bottom against the leather seat of the chair, swallowing hard as she allowed him to spread her in the chair. Her clinging, moist labia moved apart and the cool rush of air on her hot sex was a measure of how completely he had her exposed, her fragile folds—as delicate as butterfly wings—wrenched apart as she sat with her heels hooked over the arms of his chair in the middle of his living room. Half-terrified, wholly aroused, she had never felt so vulnerable, her legs spread obscenely wide, her sex laid open in erotic display as she felt the hard press of his hands on her inner thighs, urging her wider. She moaned as she felt her wet heat slide down through her crease and pool on the expensive leather beneath her.

"Don't fight me," he bit out again when her muscles tightened involuntarily. She watched his dark gaze stroke into her sex like the flick of a wet tongue and her sex jumped and blinked and gulped under the feral heat of his slow, thorough inspection. Tilting his head, his eyes glowed with a primal lust as he moved his mouth slowly toward her pussy.

His mouth was soft and warm and open as he touched her sensitive, vulnerable flesh and when her muscles clenched again, he ran his fingers down the tingling inner plane of her thighs, a firm command to relax. Twisting up inside, she tensed, waiting for the rough probe of his tongue—but it never came. Lust grew like a thick heat between her legs as his soft moist lips moved in the folds of her vagina, rubbing a kiss into her spread labia and making love to her cunt with the gentle press of his mouth as he positioned and repositioned his lips, feeding his hot breath into her pussy, an erotic wash of heat against the sensitive folds tucked inside.

Both of his thumbs were at the base of her sex, spreading her opening, tugging her wide in that terrible, wonderful stretch as he placed a long, loving kiss over her clitoris. His thumbs slipped, skidding on her slippery flesh and she knew she was creaming for the man, wet and streaming and just about a lick away from coming into his face as her slit shuddered and quivered like a trembling little mouth. When she tried to pull away from him, his strong hands tightened under her thighs, his thumbs gripping her in a cruel possessive clamp that cut into her excited flesh and almost made her come.

"Don't," he told her. He spoke the word into her wet, spread sex and the commanding word on his lips, as well as the vibration against her stretched labia, almost sent her over the edge.

"I'm ready," she gasped in a wrenching sob. "I'm ready. Please. Oh god please. I'm ready. If you don't stop, I'll come like this."

Pulling his face out of her pussy, he lifted his gaze to her eyes. "You don't want to come like this?"

Madly, she shook her head. "Do you have a condom?" she cried, hoping and praying the man was prepared.

He stood in answer, dragging a small package out of his pocket—and for the first time she saw his cock. Spearing out of his open fly, it was the most beautiful monster she'd ever seen. Huge and thick and heavy and sinfully dark, with a purple webbing of veins racing its long, entire, mouthwatering length. He stepped away from her slightly, his beige slacks low on his hips, his legs spread as he tore the package open with his teeth and let her watch him roll the latex down that incredibly long distance—from the small, neat slit in his cock head to the thick root at the base of his shaft. Then his hand returned the empty package to the pocket of his slacks, the crisp plastic crackling as he buried it deep inside.

"How do you want to be mounted?" he asked her in a hoarse rasp as he put his hands on the chair and leaned forward to touch her lips with his.

Her only answer was a groan of need.

"Do you think you could come on a rear entry?" he asked, his voice harsh and imploring, raw with lust.

"I think I could come if you...breathed on me," she confessed.

"That's my girl," he muttered in an achingly tight voice.

Lifting her out of the chair, he slipped in beneath her. With his khaki slacks pulled open and his shorts rucked down to his balls, he positioned her over the thick, heavy spike that sprang from the damp curls in his groin. "Spread your legs, April," he growled. "Wider," he ordered.

She found the back of his calves with the front of her feet as she latched on to him. Then he was shoving into her, pushing and filling and cramming into her as deep as he could get. Deliciously deep, evocatively deep, almost painfully deep, completely all-the-way-in deep, and slammed up tight against her womb. Arching with pleasure, she clasped her hands and pulled her elbows up over her head in a delicious stretch as he notched the huge bulb of his cock against her g-spot and held, seated deep inside her dark hold. Rotating her hips, she urged him deeper yet, inciting him to hammer and bruise her edge of need, hammer it into submission and release—but he remained motionless beneath her, unmoving as she sat shafted in his lap. He was packed into her, right to her limit and she had never felt so ready before in her life. She had never been so wet and open for a man—so completely *on-the-edge* prepared for orgasm.

"Want a push?" he asked her in a raw, hoarse rasp. As she moaned, trapped on the edge of ecstasy, he placed his hands on her thighs and dragged his hard fingers toward her sex. With one fingertip he prodded between her spread labia and found her clitoris. All he did was touch her. He put the tip of his finger on the ready, eager nub of her clitoris. And she came.

She went wild on him, bucking and swiveling and riding his cock as he grasped her hips and held her into the fuck, forcing her down onto his shaft as he delivered a steady, never-ending supply of steel-hard cock head tight against her g-spot. Her sluttish screams that filled the silent room were followed by wanton cries then helpless moans and finally a silky cat-like purr of contentment.

Then she realized he was still rock-hard inside her. "What about you?" she asked, feeling a little panicked over the fact that he hadn't come. Her eyes focused across the room, on the colorful pastels behind the camera, as she dragged her bottom lip through her teeth and considered the unsettling possibility that she might not have done a very good job of arousing him. "Did I do something wrong?" she asked tentatively.

She heard his tight, low laughter behind her. "Oh god, no. I'm just showing off," he told her in a taut whisper. "Trying to impress you. Believe me, I'm hanging by a thread here. The sight of you with your hands in your hair, staked out and writhing on my dick was a picture worth savoring…and keeping. The feel of you, wet and hot, your legs spread and locked wide, your pink sex open and stretched as you took in my cock and just about ate me off…" He broke off suddenly, completely still as she felt his shaft pulse deep inside the tender walls of her vagina. Carefully, he eased her off his penis.

He stood her up and turned her quickly, using his palm in the small of her back to bend her over the chair again. She settled her forearms against the chair's seat and felt the cool leather caress her hanging breasts as she turned her head.

He was waiting for her. Waiting for her to watch him mount her.

"Aren't you going to take off your slacks?" she murmured curiously.

He shook his head. "I've got a bit of a clothes fetish," he admitted around several rapid breaths. Then he grabbed the soft flesh of her ass and parted her cheeks as he penetrated her in a long, hard, unforgiving thrust. She jumped and cried out when his cock head crushed into her cervix. He started driving into her—hard—and she felt her sex opening for him again, preparing itself swiftly for a second tight orgasm. Every time he brought the huge knot of his cock head up to kiss her womb, the rough punishing contact was an instant of perfect bliss. As his thrusts became more violent she willed her sex to receive one more hit without closing up, the pleasure of near-completion so intense that she wanted it to last forever. Then he thrust and held, grinding his hips against her ass and she fell spiraling into orgasm, shouting and crying and burying her face in the chair's seat as he held her on his cock and she stood frozen in ultimate ecstasy.

Chapter Five

ꟹ

Several hours later April lay wide-awake in his bed, watching him as he slept. She was too excited to sleep, filled with bubbles again, searching for the words that would express her pleasure, knowing that only a giggle would convey the feeling of joy and contentment that built up inside her like fizzing champagne. *Here she was* lying in bed beside the most undeniably handsome man on the planet, a virtual sex god—sleeping beside him—like they were…lovers. Like they were together. A pair. A couple. A twosome!

The idea was too wonderful to contemplate.

The fact that he hadn't taken her home immediately after he'd satisfied himself on her was the icing on the cake. Lying beside him, snuggling up next to him, knowing she'd wake to his warm smile and hot male body made her want to melt with contentment and ooze happiness all over his crisp white sheets. Maybe he'd be looking for more sex in the morning. Maybe she'd get a chance to work her mouth over his cock. If she played her cards right, she might even have breakfast with him and when he finally did drive her home, maybe…just maybe…she could dare to dream he'd ask to see her again. Maybe he'd ask her what she was doing next Friday night. After all, she told herself, as she gazed at his closed eyes, the man did look as content as a man could reasonably get.

She might have dozed a few hours before dawn but April was awake again at six o'clock, waiting apprehensively for him to wake. At seven she got out of bed and took a quick shower then helped herself to a bathrobe she found hanging on the back of his bathroom door. After that, she headed for the kitchen.

* * * * *

Reaching across the bed, he searched for her, smiling. When his hands skidded across cool empty sheets, he came fully awake as he realized the space beside him was vacant. Immediately, he rolled off the bed and pulled a pair of gray sweatpants out of his top drawer. Pulling the drawstrings on his comfortable, worn sweats, he paused to check a door in the hall then continued after he'd reassured himself it was locked. He found her in the kitchen being adorably domestic, dressed in his tartan housecoat. She looked good in it. Of course that might have been due to the fact that she was bent over, rummaging through his fridge, tempting him with the very attractive sight of her upturned bottom. When she turned, she was carrying both milk and eggs. She gave him a smile as she headed back to the kitchen counter.

"Come back to bed," he told her. "I have a few more things I want to do to you this morning."

"You mean you want to do *with* me," she scolded him cheerfully as she broke two eggs into a bowl of flour.

He slouched against the doorframe, shrugging and yawning as he noted her green eyes snagged on the gray sweats hanging low on his hips. "Have it your way," he capitulated with an arched eyebrow and a smile. "Just come back to bed so I can do them to you."

"Aren't you hungry?" she questioned with a laugh. "You missed dinner last night."

"Yes, I'm hungry," he answered with a low growl. "*That's* why I want you to come back to bed."

"Just let me finish beating this," she told him as she used a whisk on the batter in the bowl. "I'm making you crepes."

"You're making me horny," he corrected her with a low laugh. He slouched over to her and pulled her into his groin as he wrapped his arms around her and cupped her breasts in his hands. "I have something here that you can beat for me," he murmured into her neck and nudged his erection against her backside to demonstrate exactly what he had in mind. "And if you're hungry, I have something you can put in your mouth, for that matter. Come back to bed and I'll let you beat me, lick me and swallow me whole."

With a giggle, she pushed her bottom into his groin and he blew out a breath of pure male satisfaction. "You smell…like morning," he told her. "Jesus, I love the way you're packaged."

"I like your package too," she quipped back at him.

"Come back to bed," he coaxed with a tongue in her ear. "And I'll let you unwrap my package. And if you're a very good girl, I'll let you keep what's inside."

When she continued to whip the thin batter, ignoring him, he snaked his hands down to the bottom of the housecoat and started working it up her legs, savoring the heat of her velvet flesh with the hard drag of his palms. "Come back to bed," he insisted. "Don't make me wait."

Pushing the dark, soft flannel up to her waist, he pulled the front of his sweatpants down and prodded his smooth cock head through her crease in a long leisurely kiss of dark male need—his hard, hungry flesh demanding a place between her soft, yielding cheeks.

"Don't make me wait," he repeated in a murmur. "I want to see my cock in your mouth." He felt her stiffen as her back curved and she fed him her plush, full bottom. His light laugh was rough with lust as his blood pounded fiercely through his veins and tightened his dick, at this point lethally hard.

Turning her with his hands on her hips, he took the whisk from her hand and laid it on the counter. Closing on her, he let his exposed, purpled cock head bob against her bared stomach before he pressed against her. With his gaze locked on hers, he collected her hair and moved it behind her shoulder.

"Would you like that?" he asked her, moving his mouth against hers and flicking his tongue over her bottom lip. "Would you like my cock in your mouth, April?" He tilted his head and watched her lower lip tremble. "Tell me what you want, baby."

Her lips moved. "I'd like that," she said in a breathless whisper.

His hands tightened on her upper arms and his tongue traveled across her mouth in a slow lick. "You'd like to suck my cock?"

Her eyes were closed when she nodded and the pink tip of her tongue ventured out to swipe at his taste, shining on her lips. "I'd like that," she croaked throatily. "I'd like to…taste you."

He prodded the pink tip of her tongue with his, moving it aside as he fed a rough breath into her mouth. "Would you like me to fuck your mouth?"

Her answer was a moan and he had to stop a moment, fighting for control, burrowing his dick into her belly, marking her with the wet prod of his weeping cock head. He felt her hand between their bodies and pulled away to watch her thumb the top of his glistening cock.

Pulling her hand away, he eased his sweatpants back up to his waist while he lifted her hand and kissed the fleshy pad of her wet thumb while holding her gaze with his.

"I want you to fuck my mouth," she told him.

"Oh, Jesus," he groaned, planting a hard, hungry kiss on her mouth, attacking her with enough energy to drive her against the counter and bend her into an erotic, womanly arch.

Leading her back through his bedroom, he continued into the bathroom, opened the shower door and pushed her in ahead of him. "Get on your knees," he told her, then turned on the water, adjusting the warm spray before he stepped in to join her. As she slid to her knees, he reached for the soap and put the bar in her hand. Standing in the middle of the black and white tiled stall, with the water spraying down on the back of his head, he reached for his drawstrings, low on his hips.

"Let me," she insisted from her place on the shower floor, reaching for the knotted strings.

"Be my guest," he told her in a tight rasp, letting her untie his sweatpants while his dick swelled in anticipation. The feel of her hands, tight against his hard, slick thighs, helping his sodden sweats down his legs didn't hurt either. His shaft sprang free with an angry bounce and he closed his eyes as the water pounded into the back of his neck and she went to work, soaping up his penis then reaching between his legs to wash his testicles.

"Oh my god," he muttered hoarsely as she continued to fondle his hardware and he continued to grow as her soapy palms slid along his shaft and cupped his balls. "I think I'm in love."

He spread his feet into a wide stance as his muscles tightened. His thighs turned to iron and his buttocks clenched into hard knots as she administered to the aching flesh growing harder yet beneath the loving caress of her artful fingers. Finally, burning at the balls and close to spilling, he pulled out of the gentle tug and stroke of her fingers, grasping his root tightly as he turned and let the water beat down on his dick, long enough to rain away the creamy white suds.

Shutting off the water with a twist of his thick wrist, he stepped out of his sopping sweatpants and turned to gaze down her. Her red hair was plastered to her head and dripping around her face as she knelt at his feet, his green housecoat wrapped around her in a wet shambles, gaping to the waist, revealing the tantalizing curves of her generous cleavage. The water beaded on her breasts and the tiny spheres collected to roll slowly between her tits.

Reaching for her chin, he tilted her face upward, gazing into her green eyes as his plum-shaped cock head rested against her cheek. The water had clumped her lashes together into dark spikes, and briefly he considered taking her mouth then and there—pushing her head to the wall as he braced his hands on the tile wall and banged his cock between her lips—and all the way down her throat.

But he knew he wouldn't last long that way. Not with the sexy little temptress on her knees before him, forced to the wall and swallowing his cock as he threw his hips at her.

And he didn't want to scare her away. He'd waited too long to get to this stage. He wasn't going to throw it all away, satisfying his own fantasies when he should be sating hers.

Pulling her to her feet, he opened the dark housecoat and pushed it off her shoulders, watching her nipples tighten as the wet flannel drooped slowly to the shower floor.

Naked and dripping wet, he led her back into his bedroom where he used his unsteady hands on her waist, guiding her to sit on the bed's edge. Kneeing her thighs apart, he pushed his legs between hers and watched her eye the fat swell of his cock head as he got his other leg between her knees and urged her thighs to open wider. Getting close to her, he moved his right leg to press against her open pussy and savored her damp heat on his thigh as his dick tightened another thick, hard degree.

He pushed out a restless, eager breath, reaching for one of her hands and wrapping it around the base of his cock as he rocked into her grip a few times. Then he used his other hand to tilt her chin as he used his fist, still wrapped around his shaft, to guide his wide cock head to her lips. He watched as she moved her mouth over his tip and put a warm suckling kiss on the smooth crown of his dick then used the tip of her tongue to track over his tight skin, lapping up his pre-cum as it bled from his slit. When she opened her mouth to take in his bulging cock head, he fed his dick between her lips, holding his breath as he watched her lips strain prettily to take his thick diameter. Gently, he thrust his hips at her mouth while she sucked at him inexpertly, her teeth often catching at the wrong place and scraping brutally at the fragile skin that cased his steel-hard erection. And when her teeth lodged several times against the sensitive wrinkled knot beneath the front rim of his cock, he found himself pulling out quickly, unwrapping her hand as he watched his dick pulse deeply, his purpled head shining with her saliva as well as a thin wash of his own seeping semen.

He stared at the sight of his huge, swollen cock head, his dick so full and taut it looked like it would explode if she so much as ran her hot little tongue up his length. When she leaned toward him with just that intent, her pink tongue flicking against her rosy lips, he yanked his hips away from her.

Eyeing his erection greedily, she got to her feet and turned as she bent forward and put her forearms on the bed. Her hair was a long wet rope sliding over one shoulder as she presented her curving bottom to him.

"Now there's a pretty sight," he rasped. Placing his palms on the back of her thighs, he dragged them up over her bottom, his hands lingering to fondle her rounded cheeks, smoothing and caressing her baby-soft skin. He gripped a handful of warm flesh in his right hand, then loosened his fingers and smoothed his hand over the pink flower his rough grip had flushed out on her flesh. "But I don't think so," he told her. "I fucked you last night. This morning I think I'll make love to you."

His hand crept between her legs, cupping her sex into his warm hold. His fingertips were tucked into the curls on her mound while the heel of his palm was nestled against the sensitive rim of her vulva.

"I love the way you fill my hand," he murmured hoarsely. "I love the way your thick pussy lips suck up to my groin and cushion my entry, surround my dick." He rubbed the fragile, damp flesh of his cock against the round curve of her cheeky ass while he gripped her bottom firmly and started to move the fingers of his other hand—the hand that cupped her pussy possessively.

Fingering his way between the plump lips of her labia, he stroked through her rutted folds a few times, finally settling on a rumpled little knot of flesh. She gasped when he dragged his fingertip over the feminine little pearl. "Eureka," he muttered. "I've hit gold."

He continued to grip and knead her bottom while he used his fingers on her clitoris, pulling small choking gasps out of her mouth along with small whimpering moans, all the while wiping his hot, aching flesh against her pale bottom, watching a shining wash of semen stream from the slit in his cock head to coat the top of his dick.

He was getting dangerously close.

"Fuck," he whispered in a heavy groan, finally pulling his fingers down through her folds to test her opening. "Fuck," he whispered darkly when he found the entrance to her cunt primed—slippery and hot, begging for his penetration. He slipped his finger into her wet heat, up to the first joint, and felt her sex flutter hungrily to kiss his finger. She was so ready for him. Ready to be shafted. "Fuck," he murmured a third time.

He heard her light laugh. "Well, get on with it then."

"Oh god," he gave her a strained laugh in return. "You're asking for it, lady."

With a hand gripping her hip, he twisted her quickly to sit on the bed as he reached for his slacks on the end of the mattress. Digging into the pocket, he retrieved a square package and put it in her hands. "Open it," he told her. "No. With your teeth." When she'd torn an opening into the plastic, she drew the latex condom into her hand as he nudged his streaming cock head against her cheek. "Put it on me," he directed her then watched her get it started over the broad, dark head of his pulsing dick. At that point, he stopped her with a fist under her chin. "Put it on me," he said again in a voice like polished steel, "with your mouth."

When she gave him a hesitant look of uncertainty, he nodded down on her. "Use your mouth, April." Then he watched with heated interest as her plump lips slid over the head then started to push the rolled ridge of latex down his vein-rich shaft. Halfway down his length, she got hung up and he held the back of her head as he pushed into her mouth, forcing the condom another inch farther along his rod before withdrawing his cock and using his fingers to roll the remaining latex down to cover his thick root.

Then he pushed her over with two hands on her shoulders and climbed on top of her, spreading her thighs with his knees, pulling her legs up beside his body as he found her notch and shoved into her pussy.

Oh god, she was hot!

He felt her tender opening choke around his entry and he restrained the urge to dig in deep, waiting for her body to accept his first penetration before carefully feeding her a few more inches—though his muscles strained and sweat dampened the dark spray of hair in his armpits.

"Come on, April," he beseeched her with a tempered snarl. "Let me in, sweetheart. I won't hurt you," he groaned. "I promise I won't hurt you. Just ease up, darling."

His cock dragged inside her steamy tight channel and finally he found the way to the back of her cunt. Catching her knees inside his elbows, he urged them higher and almost came when her knees dropped laterally toward the bed. Her cunt relaxed, her body relaxed and when he started to ride into her, she was like an animal beneath him, her body rising to meet him thrust for thrust as she bucked on the bed and ground against him. When she started to scream, his balls tightened and he began to come. And come. And come. And come. The searing, scalding pleasure that swamped his sex rocked him to his soul as he crammed his cock deep inside the tight grip of her spasming cunt and shot into her in long, satisfying surges.

When he finally finished inside her and lifted his head to gaze at her through the sweat-dampened strands of his dark hair, he found her with her teeth buried in the full pad of her bottom lip. With a groan, he kissed her.

As he took her lips, there was a rustle of cloth and a small thud as he vaguely noted his slacks had slid off the end of the bed where he'd thrown them earlier.

* * * * *

It was amazing what a contented creature man was after a little sex, April decided, sitting on the bed's edge and watching him. He was on his back. His eyes were closed and his arms were flung over his head, revealing the spray of male hair caught in the cup of his armpits. Standing, she reached for his slacks, crumpled on the floor, shaking them and folding them before returning them to the end of the bed. Scuffing across the bedroom she kicked something across the hardwood floor and scooped it up, checking it out as she headed down the hall toward the kitchen.

It had obviously fallen from the pocket of his slacks, she decided. It looked like some sort of remote control although it was a bit on the small side. Reaching the kitchen, she slapped it down on the counter and noticed the manufacturer's name embossed in gold letters on black plastic. Nikon. It was the name of a camera. As she stood at the kitchen counter, her eyes cut immediately to the camera in the living room. Mounted on a tripod, the lens cap was off and the camera's aperture was pointed at the large leather chair on the opposite side of the room.

All at once, April felt terribly ill. The remote had obviously fallen from the pocket of his slacks—the same slacks he'd worn the whole time they were on the chair together, last night. Creeping fearfully around the counter, she glanced down the hallway toward the bedroom door then continued on to inspect the digital camera. It took her a few seconds to power it up but when she had the camera turned on and had the small display screen pulled out, the first thing she saw was the first picture he'd taken.

One hand was across her mouth and the other clutched her belly as her stomach tightened into sick knots. He'd photographed her on the chair. She backed away from the tripod, tripping over her feet as she fought to distance herself from the cold, hard, colorful fact revealed in the camera's small square display window. He'd photographed her on the chair…without her knowledge.

Steeling herself, she stepped back to the tripod, fingers shaking as they slid over the black camera, trying to find the advance button. The first picture showed the full length of her body, from head to toe, standing in front of the chair, looking over her shoulder as she pulled down her zipper. Any pictures he took after that would be a good deal more explicit. She searched for the advance button while she worried about locating the delete button at the same time.

There was a rustle of sound from the bedroom and she stared down the hall, holding her breath. Another noise followed and she froze a moment in indecision. Then, hurrying across the room, she found her panties tucked beneath the front edge of the chair. Retrieving them, she slid into her rumpled dress, still puddled on the floor.

She felt something hot slide down her cheek. Unsympathetically, she brushed the tear away with the back of her wrist. *Move,* she told herself. *Move. Get out before the bastard wakes to find you crying like a helpless idiot.*

Briefly, she pictured him trying to explain. His hands on her, restraining her, as he attempted to reassure her. Her stomach turned at the thought of his hands on her again.

She'd smash the damn camera, but then he'd have a reason to set the police after her. And she didn't want him to find her. Ever again. That's all she could think of. She didn't want to see him and she didn't want him to find her. Reaching for his blazer on the couch, she took his car keys from his pocket.

*****

A quiet click snapped him out of his contented lassitude. Raising himself on one elbow, he called her name tentatively as a sudden sense of unease bore down on him with the weight of stiff, wet concrete. He rolled off the bed and started across the room, pulling his khaki slacks up his legs as he strode through his bedroom door, palming his cock to one side and zipping his fly as he headed down the hall. He froze when he saw his small black remote on the kitchen counter.

Cutting a glance into the foyer, he shot across the living room, rotating his camera and finding it powered up. "Fuck!" he spat out, racing out of the room then over the cold stone tiles in the foyer, tearing the door open as he vaulted down the steps into his yard. Spinning like a periscope in the middle of the lawn, he found no trace of her. "Fuck," he groaned, throwing his head back and ripping his hands back through his hair in anguish as he stared at his car parked against the curb.

Tearing back to the house again, he smashed his toe on the stone steps leading up to his front door. He left a trail of blood to mark his return to the living room, going through the pockets of his blazer as his long legs took him back through the foyer. Suddenly realizing his keys weren't in the pocket of his jacket, he threw the coat to the tiled floor. Frantically, he plunged his hands into the side pockets of his pants in a frenzied search that produced nothing.

"Oh no," he breathed. "Oh no," he moaned as he paced back through the living room, searching countertop and floor and table top for his keys. And then he realized. She'd done something with his keys. She must have taken them with her. Or hidden them. Or flushed them down the toilet!

In a black frustration of dark emotion he stood—locked in helpless rage. Then he started shouting. Shouting at himself. Two years gone to fucking hell! Two years he'd worked to convince her she should go out with him and he'd fucking blown it on the very first date.

Finally he acted, although he knew he'd be an hour behind her. But he knew where she worked and he knew where she lived. With this knowledge to sustain him, he tore through the phone book, located a phone number and called a cab.

Chapter Six

ℬ

The keys turned up at the bottom of the kitchen sink, within the dark recesses of the garbage disposal. Unfortunately, he didn't discover that fact until he used the garbage disposal a week after their date. It destroyed the disposal unit and chewed up his keys. But by then he'd picked up his second set from his studio in the city.

He tried everything to find her—everything short of a full-page ad. She'd left her job at the convenience store without notice. Worse than that, her manager had refused to give him either a phone number or address for her, explaining that it was against company policy.

There was no answer when he knocked at her apartment door. Knowing that she'd recognize his vehicle, he rented a car and sat outside her apartment for two days, hoping to catch her either coming or going. But she'd evidently abandoned her rental as well—and nobody came to empty her mailbox or pick up the newspapers that piled up on her doorstep. He'd talked to the apartment manager, but the overly protective old hen had refused to offer any information other than the fact that number 217 was not available for rent.

He remembered that her mother lived in Phippsburg and he checked the telephone directory, only to realize he didn't know April's last name. Kicking himself for all the wasted hours he'd spent saying the wrong things and asking the wrong questions when he could have learned more about her, he checked the phone book anyway, on the off-chance that her last name was actually April. There were no Aprils listed in either the local phone book or the directory that covered the small towns on the city's outskirts.

Leaving his work, he drove over to Phippsburg and prowled the town, then parked at the local grocery store for a day. It was the only grocery store in town and she might have turned up there, had he been lucky. But luck had apparently deserted him, quite as cleanly as she, herself, had evaded him.

Returning to the city, he spent another several days haunting the street outside her apartment building. After ten days, he was pretty certain the post office was forwarding her mail—because the colored envelopes that he was sending her weren't in the mailman's hand when he pushed junk mail into her mailbox. Restless at the end of the day, he often found himself parked again on the street outside her apartment, gazing blankly at her unlit windows as night moved across the sky and darkened the city streets as well as his mood.

After two weeks, he had gone back to work.

* * * * *

Dalton Cristofer tilted his head as he considered the pastel before him. Reaching out with a stained thumb, he dragged the digit a careful centimeter across the surface of the canvas. There was a sound behind him but he didn't turn.

"Don't you answer your door anymore?" a man's voice queried at his back.

"Was that you knocking?" Dalton asked vaguely.

"You call that knocking? I thought Rob was going to put his fist through the door!"

Repositioning his thumb slightly, Dalton spoke without turning. "What are you doing here, Bret?"

"Just checking on you. Your phone's broken."

"Is it?"

"You tell me. Nobody's heard from you in...weeks."

A short silence followed.

"You okay?"

Using his wrist to hitch at his sweatpants, Dalton frowned as he stared at the canvas.

A second man's voice echoed down the hall. "D'you find him?"

"In here," Bret called out. "Did you put the key back?"

"Under the rock," Rob told him as he entered the room. There was a rustling clink of glass and cardboard then a cold beer was in Dalton's hand. Without thinking, he lifted it to his lips.

"Who is she?" Rob asked, standing beside him and lifting his own beer toward the canvas.

"April." More silence followed as Dalton hitched his sweatpants up his hips again.

"When's the last time you ate?" Rob asked quietly.

Dalton swallowed a mouthful of beer and shook his head.

"When's the last time you shaved," Rob went on with a prod, "or showered for that matter? Or changed that T-shirt?"

"I don't know!" Dalton suddenly exploded, turning so quickly that beer flew from the mouth of the brown bottle in his fist. It left a shining arc on the studio floor. "When's the last time you wrote a decent book?" Glaring at the two men, Dalton caught Bret's wince. Bret's long square mouth flattened as his worried brown eyes flicked to the man beside him. But the reaction Dalton expected from the normally incendiary Rob didn't happen.

Pulling a restraining hand through his black hair, Rob cut a frown at Bret then at his angry friend. "What's wrong, man?"

Dalton turned to face the windows on the south wall of his home studio, downing his bottle of beer in several large swallows. "I fucked up," he told them in a low voice, throwing his bottle four feet into a metal wastebasket against the wall. The bottle hit the can with a vicious, rattling clang. "I *really* fucked up," he said mournfully, dropping onto a high stool as he turned to face his friends.

"Is this about art?" Bret queried carefully, his eyes narrowed on the canvas. "Or is this about a woman?"

Dalton grimaced as he pulled his open hand down over his short, soft beard. "Both."

"Order some food," Rob instructed Bret. His diamond blue eyes settled on Dalton. "That Chinese place still delivers, doesn't it?"

Dalton nodded as Bret pulled his cell phone out of his pocket. Punching in C H I - N E S E, he flipped his brown hair out of the way before putting the phone to his ear.

"Okay," Rob told him. "Start talking."

* * * * *

"Send her the pastel," Rob told him when Dalton had finished relating his story. The three friends were sprawled across Dalton's living room. The low table in front of his leather couch was littered with the standing dead—empty beer bottles—as well as an assortment of well-ravaged take-out containers. Bret and Rob shared the couch, while Dalton slouched in the wide-armed chair.

With a crisp fragment of sesame beef on the end of his fork, Bret pointed the utensil at Dalton. "Is that the chair?" he asked with a taunting grin.

Glaring at Bret, Dalton pressed his lips together.

"Send her the canvas," Rob repeated. "It's the only thing she can't ignore."

Dalton rolled his shoulders tensely. "I'm showing the series in a week."

"She'll bring it back."

Dalton considered Rob's face worriedly then swung his gaze to Bret.

"Send her the canvas," Bret agreed with a reassuring smile. "Along with an invitation to your showing."

Reluctantly, Dalton nodded. He lifted his chin. "I can't believe you guys flew out here."

Bret shrugged. "We hadn't heard from you. We were worried. You know how artists are—*dark*," he taunted, "*moody*. Liable to throw themselves off of cliffs when things don't go their way," he pointed out cheerfully.

Dalton shot him a half-hearted grin.

"Besides," Rob added. "We still owe you for dragging us through History of Art in our freshman year at CU."

"And graphic design," Bret put in.

Dalton snorted. "Not to mention geometry," he reminded them snidely.

Rob lifted his chin with sudden interest, a warm smile lighting his fierce blue gaze. "Geometry," he said slowly and both men knew what he was thinking. "Miss Masters," he drawled, "She was hot. I wouldn't have minded bisecting her arcs."

Bret looked surprised. "I thought you did!"

Rob shook his head with an evil grin. "I came close," he offered amiably. "But close only counts in—"

"Hand grenades," Dalton finished for him.

"And slow dancing," Bret added with a pleasant smile.

Rob lifted his beer bottle. "To Miss Masters," he suggested philosophically. "And women of the same ilk. Women with arcs and curves and great, round circumferences."

Lifting their beers in solemn respect, Dalton and Bret joined Rob in his toast then downed the contents of their bottles.

Chapter Seven

ꝏ

Almost a month after his disastrous experience with April, Dalton Cristofer was standing in the middle of his studio on Main Street. A frenetic collection of recent hits played over the sound system. Rob had burned the CD for him before he'd left for his home in California. It wasn't loud, but it was intense. Like Rob. Right now, it matched his mood. As he watched the studio's glass door with the keen interest of a predatory hawk, people laughed and talked as they moved around him, sipping their wine and following a winding path through the canvases he was showing.

Surely she'd come.

The door to his studio opened and he smiled impatiently at the young couple who stepped inside, his head tilting to search behind them. He heard his name and dragged his eyes from the door.

An older woman, tall and elegant, had just finished her round of the dozen canvases, each of which was named for a different month of the year, and every one depicting a square snippet of a woman's body. Each window of art included a flesh tone, from ivory to ebony, along with two additional colors—a fragment of the model's dress as well as a sweep of the model's hair.

"This is brilliant, Dalton," she told him. Her once-blonde hair was pulled back in a tight knot. The severe hairstyle went hand in hand with her black tailored suit. "Absolutely brilliant. I predict your "Evening Gown Collection" will outsell everything you've done to date. Do you plan to offer the pieces individually or as a set?"

He shrugged, not actually looking at her, his eyes returning to the door.

"What about this one in the center of the room?"

"April," he stated. "It's a working copy," he told her tersely, pulling a stick of gum from his pocket and unwrapping it before he fed the powdery length into his mouth. "I'm waiting for the finished art to arrive. I'm hoping it will be here before the end of the night."

"You look tired," the elegant woman admonished him gently.

He nodded, glancing at her before returning his eyes to the door. "It was a bit of a rush," he admitted, "trying to get all of this ready in time."

She had to come, he told himself. She had to come. Even if she'd ignored the twenty-odd notes he'd sent her, she couldn't ignore the package he'd mailed. But that was six days ago, and he'd sent it priority. Inwardly, he groaned.

He couldn't believe he'd blown it. After two years of careful encouragement, trying to convince her to give him a chance, he'd thrown it all away in one stupid, careless act. Wrapped up in his own needs, wants and ambitions—more concerned with his own desires than April's need to feel secure with a man she'd only just begun to trust—he'd carelessly risked and ultimately squandered the interest of the one woman who truly captivated him.

Surely she'd come.

But at the end of the evening, as his last guest made her goodbyes, the working copy was still on display instead of the final version he'd hoped would arrive to take its place.

"Thanks for coming, Clarisse," he told the older woman, dropping a light kiss on her powdered cheek as he pushed the door open for her.

"Get some rest," she told him with a sympathetic smile.

"I will," he promised, stepping outside with her as he glanced up and down the sidewalk that paralleled the neat line of exclusive shops on Main Street. But the street was dark and empty.

With a sigh, he stepped back into his studio and let the door close behind him.

Dragging a folding chair into the center of the room, he dropped into it, slouching disconsolately as he stared at the working pastel. His cock stirred with an unhappy twinge and he sighed. "I miss her too," he muttered under his breath. "I only took one," he said darkly.

"I only took one picture," he insisted in a black mutter, leaning forward with his elbows on his knees. He held his head as he stared at the floor.

"*I only took one picture*!" he shouted, standing suddenly and whipping the chair across the studio to crash into the wall. Several framed originals trembled in place, shivering against the wall as he stared at them. There was a small scrape of noise behind him and he spun angrily.

And there she stood.

He hadn't heard the door open, but then a folding chair makes a lot of noise when it smashes against a wall. He glared at her. "I only took *one* picture," he grated. "That one!" He flung his hand behind him to point at the canvas honoring the stand in the center of the lighted room.

She held a large, flat package under her arm. With a sad, wry expression, she considered the working pastel for a moment before her eyes drifted down to the stand upon which it was displayed. "That's a lot of cigarette packages," she told him, staring glumly at the tall, rectangular pedestal he'd built from the small green cigarette boxes. "Are the cigarettes still…"

"I told you I didn't smoke," he blasted back at her.

She shook her head. "I'm sorry," she said, "but that damn remote was in your pocket the whole time you were…we were…"

"I have a bit of a clothes fetish!" he almost exploded, his hands balling at his sides. "Is that so bad?"

Again she shook her head, apologetically. "And the locked door in the hall? That's your…"

"Home studio," they said together.

She nodded bleakly. "I got your invitation," she said in a small voice, extending the package toward him. "Why didn't you just tell me?" she queried reasonably.

"You didn't give me a *chance*!" he ripped into her, grabbing the package out of her hands and pulling the box apart, then tearing the cardboard away to reach his art inside.

"No. I mean, why didn't you tell me you were going to photograph me…for this?"

His jaw dropped as he considered her question with open frustration. "You can't get a candid shot when the subject knows the camera is on her. You can't get…anything real."

"Why didn't you tell me afterward, then?"

Turning, he replaced the working copy with the finished product. "It was going to be a surprise," he muttered sulkily. "I was going to bring you here…on a date. To this showing," he added in a low voice. He settled the picture into its clear glass easel and waved his hand at it. "It was going to be a surprise," he finished without energy.

"It was a surprise all right," she smiled sadly. Her gaze swung to the oil pastel and she moved toward it. "It's beautiful," she told him, joining him as he considered his work.

Within the small square of canvas, he'd presented the lower half of her face, turned as she looked over her shoulder. Her teeth were pressed into the luscious shine of her full bottom lip. The clean, sharp sweep of her black gown descended down over her shoulder and disappeared at the bottom edge of the canvas. On the other side of the canvas, her long fall of flaming hair paralleled the plunging line of her black dress. "It's perfect," he told her.

"You should have *known,*" he stated in a voice gravelly with emotion. "You should have *known* I wouldn't have done something like that to you…to *anyone*. I wouldn't photograph you without your knowledge. Not like that. Not naked and spread across my chair. At least, not without your permission," he grumbled. "What kind of man do you think I am?" He blew out a sigh as he slid a look sideways at her. "Where have you been? Didn't you get my letters?"

She shrugged as her gaze settled on the floor. "I didn't believe any of it until I got your art in the mail," she told him. "That was this morning. I've been staying with my mother out in Phippsburg. My mail is being forwarded but…the post office is a bit small out there. They're…not all that efficient."

"I told you I was an artist," he said. "In my letters! At least twenty-one times."

She nodded. "Twenty-three times."

"Why did you find that so hard to believe? Didn't you check me out? I'm on the net!" he argued. "I even uploaded a recent picture so that you'd recognize me!"

"My mother doesn't have a computer," she shot back defensively.

"And Phippsburg doesn't have a library?"

"I didn't believe you!" She was suddenly yelling at him. "I didn't get online to check you out because I didn't believe you and I didn't want to think about you! I didn't believe you were Dalton. I thought…Dalton was the artist's *last* name. Everybody does! And *your* last name is Cristofer!"

He stared at her for more than a second. "I'm sorry," he said finally. "Jesus. I'm sorry, April."

She considered his troubled face as he dragged his hands back through his hair, his lips turning downward as he blew out a hard sigh. "Besides," she complained in a forgiving grumble. "You don't look like an artist."

"What do you mean?"

Tilting her head, she considered his face. "You're so…masculine," she tried to explain. "Your face. Your hands. Even your wrists are…so thick. You don't look like an artist is supposed to look.

"And even if I had thought you *looked* like an artist, you don't act like one. You're so…*earthy*. In your needs. So primal. So male."

Moving away from him, she wandered across the studio, stopping to consider one square canvas featuring a very long, very black neck leading to soft draping folds of white. The picture revealed a small amount of smooth, thick hair pulled away from the model's neck. "January," she said, reading the title card below the canvas. *Blackberry*, she thought.

She stepped across the room and tilted her head to consider a rain of gold hair curling over the top of a shining, strapless dress. The dress was fire engine red and obviously vinyl. "March," she said, then murmured quietly to herself, "Strawberry ripple. Isn't this…" she lifted her questioning eyes to his.

He nodded, "One of my models. You might have seen me with her."

"Was she *only* a model?"

"I don't like to use professional models for my work," he explained. "They're too…slick. And they're usually too…perfect. As a rule, I'm looking for something different in a model. It might be the way she twists her hands together or the way she winds her hair around her finger." He gazed again at the pastel in the center of the room. "Something different in action or expression. When I find an interesting subject, I try to get a candid shot. If I get something I think I can use, I share the photograph with the subject and ask her if she'd like to sell me the shot. If she agrees, I pay her."

Returning to stand beside him, she gazed again at her own likeness. "Orange sherbet," she murmured, feeling a little proud. "How much is your standard rate?"

"It varies," he admitted then took a deep breath. "I won't pretend I haven't slept with some of these women. Some of them wouldn't accept anything for the pictures."

"You've had sex with some of them. Have you ever made love to any of them?" she asked.

"No," he said quietly. "Not really."

She smiled minutely. "Well," she told him, feeling a fraction bolder, "you owe me for the shot, don't you?"

He nodded without saying anything.

"What's the going rate?" she asked again.

He rolled one shoulder. "A thousand."

"Do you mean to say," she pretended to look surprised as she turned toward him, "that you're going to have sex with me a thousand times?"

Finally his grim expression gave way to a smile and she smiled back.

"I'm kidding," she admitted finally. "I don't expect anything for the photograph. I had a lovely time with you. I apologize for the misunderstanding. I'm sorry I didn't get your artwork back in time for the showing." With those words, she extended her hand as a final peace offering. "Thank you, Mr. Dalton Cristofer, for including me in your series." When he made no move to shake her hand and she realized he wasn't going to accept her apology, she watched her hand blur behind rippling tears. Slowly, she dropped her arm and turned toward the door.

"Where do you think you're going?" he asked her.

She shrugged as she hurried toward the exit.

"April. Where are you going? After all of this, you expect me to shake hands and say goodbye? Excuse me if I'm a bit stunned. Too stunned to shake your hand. Let me catch up," he insisted, following her and grasping her arm, spinning her to face him.

"You got your picture and I got a wonderful night," she explained with a lopsided lift of her shoulder.

"Have you forgotten that I had an ulterior motive when I invited you to my home?"

"I thought…the picture was the ulterior motive."

"The pastel? Hell no! What kind of ulterior motive would that be? I invited you to my home so I could get you into my bedroom and get you stripped down and live out every carnal fantasy I've ever had since I met you…every one of which included you. So that I could do to you all the things I've dreamed of since I first met you.

"I've never had trouble finding women, April. Even when I was a kid in high school. What I had trouble finding was a woman who could hold her own with me. Who could fling it back as fast as I could dish it out. When I walked into the convenience store two years ago and bought a pack of gum and started giving the girl behind the counter a hard time, I just about swallowed my gum when she had a clever comeback.

"That was you," he said softly. "While I was trying to think of what to say next, I ordered the cigarettes…just so I could watch you reach over your head for them." A guilty smile softened his features. "Just so I could watch your breasts bounce," he admitted.

"I didn't stop smiling all of that first day. I pulled out a canvas when I got to my studio and started a new work. For the first time in my life, I could do nothing wrong. It was like I'd found my muse or something. Everything I've put together since that day has been a huge success. Just because you keep me smiling.

"So if you think you're going to shake my hand and walk out that door, Miss April, you can just think again."

"You want to be friends?"

He almost gagged. "Friends!" he choked. "No! I don't want to be friends. Don't you get it, April? I *want* you! I want *you*."

"You want me to be your…'flavor of the month'?" she asked with shy hope.

"'Flavor of the month'?" he shouted at her, shaking his head, obviously confused.

She nodded minutely, her teeth in her bottom lip. "Like the others," she indicated with a flick of her head. "Strawberry and blackberry."

"Strawberry and… January and March?" His eyes narrowed on the pastels she indicated then returned to her face. "Yeah," he said. "Yeah. I'd like that. I've always had a thing for orange. How would you feel about being my 'flavor of a lifetime', Miss April?"

"'Flavor of a lifetime'?" she queried in a very faint voice.

"Yeah," he answered, "'flavor of a lifetime'—as in orange sherbet for the rest of my life. Because I'm thinking there won't be any other 'flavors of the month' for me. And if that sounds good to you, we'll see what we can do about changing your name at the same time," he murmured as he closed on her.

"Changing my name?" she queried with an arched brow while backing away from him but wisely making her way toward the wall.

He nodded as he pinned her to the wall with the long, powerful length of his body. "Changing your name, *Miss April*. It really doesn't suit you."

"Oh? And exactly what do you think would suit better?"

"I was thinking of something more along the lines of Mrs. Cristofer," he murmured against the warm column of her neck.

"Mrs. Cristofer?"

Again, he nodded. "Mrs. Dalton Cristofer. I love you, April. If I didn't know it before, I do now. These past few weeks have been…hard. If I hadn't had your picture and your pastel to work on…I don't know what I would have done. I just kept working on your mouth—long after it was finished and perfect—dragging my thumb over your bottom lip, rubbing more color into it." By now, his thumb was against her damp lips, stroking over the tingling surface of her open mouth.

"But we've only known each other—"

He cut her off. "Two years, four months and two days," he told her gently.

She reached for his wrist, checking his watch. "Ten hours and twenty-eight minutes," she added in a scolding tone.

Laughing, he pulled her into his arms. "So what do you say, Miss April? Are you going to let me make love to you for the rest of my life?"

"That sounds all right," she challenged him with a stern smile. "Although I'd prefer it if we could make love *to each other* for the rest of our lives."

He growled at her as his lips kicked up into a smile and his eyes glowed with love as well as lust. “Oh, all right. Have it your way.”

About the Author

ꕥ

I slung the heavy battery pack around my hips and cinched it tight – or tried to. "Damn." Brian grabbed an awl. Leaning over me, he forged a new hole in the too-big belt. "Any advice?" I asked him as I pulled the belt tight. "Yeah. Don't reach for the ore cart until it starts moving, then jump on the back and immediately duck your head. The voltage in the overhead cable won't just kill you. It'll blow you apart."

That was my first day on my first job. Employed as an engineer, I've worked in an underground mine that went up—inside a mountain. I've swung over the Ohio River in a tiny cage suspended from a crane in the middle of an electrical storm. I've hung over the Hudson River at midnight in an aluminum boat—30 foot in the air—suspended from a floating barge at the height of a blizzard, while snowplows on the bridge overhead rained slush and salt down on my shoulders. You can't do this sort of work without developing a sense of humor, and a sense of adventure.

New to publishing, I read my first romance two years ago and started writing. Both my reading and writing habits are subject to mood and I usually have several stories going at once. When I need a really good idea for a story, I clean toilets. Now there's an activity that engenders escapism.

I was surveying when I met my husband. He was my 'rod man'. While I was trying to get my crosshairs on his stadia rod, he dropped his pants and mooned me. Next thing I know, I've got the backside of paradise in my viewfinder. So I grabbed the walkie-talkie. "That's real nice," I told him, "but would you please turn around? I'd rather see the other side."

…it was love at first sight.

Madison welcomes comments from readers. You can find her website and email address on her author bio page at www.ellorascave.com.

Why an electronic book?

We live in the Information Age—an exciting time in the history of human civilization, in which technology rules supreme and continues to progress in leaps and bounds every minute of every day. For a multitude of reasons, more and more avid literary fans are opting to purchase e-books instead of paper books. The question from those not yet initiated into the world of electronic reading is simply: *Why?*

1. ***Price.*** An electronic title at Ellora's Cave Publishing and Cerridwen Press runs anywhere from 40% to 75% less than the cover price of the exact same title in paperback format. Why? Basic mathematics and cost. It is less expensive to publish an e-book (no paper and printing, no warehousing and shipping) than it is to publish a paperback, so the savings are passed along to the consumer.
2. ***Space.*** Running out of room in your house for your books? That is one worry you will never have with electronic books. For a low one-time cost, you can purchase a handheld device specifically designed for e-reading. Many e-readers have large, convenient screens for viewing. Better yet, hundreds of titles can be stored within your new library—on a single microchip. There are a variety of e-readers from different manufacturers. You can also read e-books on your PC or laptop computer. (Please note that Ellora's

Cave does not endorse any specific brands. You can check our websites at www.ellorascave.com or www.cerridwenpress.com for information we make available to new consumers.)

3. ***Mobility***. Because your new e-library consists of only a microchip within a small, easily transportable e-reader, your entire cache of books can be taken with you wherever you go.
4. ***Personal Viewing Preferences.*** Are the words you are currently reading too small? Too large? Too... ANNOYING? Paperback books cannot be modified according to personal preferences, but e-books can.
5. ***Instant Gratification.*** Is it the middle of the night and all the bookstores near you are closed? Are you tired of waiting days, sometimes weeks, for bookstores to ship the novels you bought? Ellora's Cave Publishing sells instantaneous downloads twenty-four hours a day, seven days a week, every day of the year. Our webstore is never closed. Our e-book delivery system is 100% automated, meaning your order is filled as soon as you pay for it.

Those are a few of the top reasons why electronic books are replacing paperbacks for many avid readers.

As always, Ellora's Cave and Cerridwen Press welcome your questions and comments. We invite you to email us at Comments@ellorascave.com or write to us directly at Ellora's Cave Publishing Inc., 1056 Home Avenue, Akron, OH 44310-3502.

Cerridwen, the Celtic Goddess of wisdom, was the muse who brought inspiration to storytellers and those in the creative arts. Cerridwen Press encompasses the best and most innovative stories in all genres of today's fiction. Visit our site and discover the newest titles by talented authors who still get inspired - much like the ancient storytellers did, once upon a time.

ELLORA'S CAVE
ROMANTICA PUBLISHING